I0825441

THE TOMBSTONE TRAIL

Also by Ray Hogan and available from Center Point Large Print:

The Crosshatch Men
Pilgrim
The Renegade Gun
Betrayal in Tombstone
Highroller's Man
Omaha Crossing
Honeymaker's Son

THE TOMBSTONE TRAIL

A Shawn Starbuck Western

RAY HOGAN

CENTER POINT LARGE PRINT
THORNDIKE, MAINE

This Center Point Large Print edition
is published in the year 2026 by arrangement with
Golden West Inc.

First published by Signet Books.

The text of this Large Print edition is unabridged.
In other aspects, this book may vary
from the original edition.
Printed in the United States of America
on permanent paper sourced using
environmentally responsible foresting methods.
Set in 16-point Times New Roman type.

ISBN: 979-8-90082-027-9

The Library of Congress has cataloged this record
under Library of Congress Control Number: 2026935575

ONE

Starbuck, on his haunches in the welter of rocks and growth at the foot of Arizona's Whetstone Mountains, drew to sudden alert. Off to his left, the brush had rattled, and in a land being ravaged fiercely by Victorio's renegade Apaches, every unaccounted-for sound was suspect.

Putting aside the hard biscuit and strip of jerky on which he was making a tasteless supper, he dropped a hand to the heavy forty-five Colt hung low on his left thigh. Taut, he turned carefully and faced the direction of the noise. A dozen steps away, the big sorrel gelding he rode was dozing wearily in a stand of junipers, almost but not entirely hidden by the gray-green foliage. Earlier, he had sought to better conceal the horse but found it impossible in the stunted growth.

Easing forward, Shawn moved silently to the edge of the small clearing in which he had made camp, ears cocked for a repeat of the sound, eyes probing the surrounding shrubbery. It was still an hour or more until sunset, and much too early to halt for the night, but he'd come a long way that day—nearly the distance from Tucson—and with Apaches on the prowl, it was only good sense to expose oneself as little as possible.

All things being equal, he should have reached

the booming new silver town of Tombstone that morning, but the trail he'd been forced to take because of the marauding Indians had swung him far to the west and thrown him hours behind.

Not that there was any great haste to reach the settlement, still only six months old and rising to prominence on the shoulders of the rich strikes being made in the dark San Pedro hills. One day, two—or a week late—it mattered little, since his mission was simply one of search and just one more leg in a so far fruitless quest for his brother, Ben.

Ben, who also called himself Damon Friend, might logically be expected to be in Tombstone. Since he was a footloose wanderer—never staying in one place, as Starbuck had long since learned—the fabulous fledgling town pouring out its endless wealth would prove to be as irresistible to men such as he as had been the fabled Sirens to the sailors of ancient Greece.

Shawn had been in Dodge City, to which he had guided the last of three Mexican vaqueros in an attempt to recover money taken from them, when he first heard of Tombstone. The word there was that every fiddle foot west of the Missouri and quite a few to the east of the big river had taken to the trail for the Arizona El Dorado, even Wyatt Earp, with whom he'd become acquainted during other visits to the boisterous cow town.

Earp, he surmised, would probably again pin

on a star and go about the deadly business of bringing law and order to the roaring settlement, something reported to be absolutely nonexistent by those who had been there. It wouldn't take the cool, gray-eyed Earp long to accomplish the task, Shawn reckoned; he had done it before in other tough towns, and he no doubt could do it again . . . He'd seek out the lawman first thing, renew acquaintances, and then ask him about Ben. Earp had that faculty of being aware of all things and all persons once he took over.

Starbuck relaxed slowly, drew back to the far side of the clearing. The rustling sound had not come again. Likely, it was some small animal moving about in the dry leaves and dead branches in search of food. A few minutes before, he had noticed an owl staring wide-eyed at him from a nearby tree; chances were the bird had been drawn there by that same animal—a rabbit or perhaps a ground squirrel.

Again squatting, Shawn resumed eating his meal, munching on the biscuit, tearing bits of the dry, salty beef from a strip with his teeth, chewing patiently, and finally washing all down with a swallow of water from his canteen. He would have enjoyed a good supper that night, one of fresh meat stew and hot coffee, since he had not treated himself to such in two days; but a fire meant not only smoke but a widely drifting odor as well and either would attract Apaches.

Hunger satisfied, he rose, hung the canteen on a stump of ragged mesquite, and looked out over the long slope that flowed down to the valley below. There was a distinct coolness in the air, normal, he supposed, for late October, despite the fact that he was in the upper reaches of the Sonoran Desert. Altitude made the difference, he guessed, and realized he could expect the nights to become much sharper as the months progressed.

But he didn't plan to stay that long in Tombstone. If, after a time, he failed to locate Ben or turn up any word on him, he'd move on. There would be little to appeal to him in a mining town; he was a farm boy turned cowhand and trail rider, and digging into the bowels of the earth, however lucrative, was not his idea of a life.

Perhaps he'd ride on down into Mexico, seek out the area from which his three vaquero friends had come. Or he just might head north, go on up into Oregon. He'd not been that far northwest yet, and the chances that Ben would be found there were no worse or better than in any other part of the country.

He would have to find work, raise a few dollars, though. The trip to Dodge with the Mexicans, during which he had used his own meager capital on the strength of being paid for his services once they collected what was due them, had ended in failure, and he was out the cash outlay.

The loss of the money had not particularly disturbed him; money was only money, something a man made use of when it became necessary, but his reduced funds were an inconvenience and meant that, as on many previous occasions, he would be compelled to abandon the search for Ben and take time to replenish his poke.

Mesilla . . . Maybe he had best make that settlement his next destination if he drew a blank in Tombstone. The last trace he'd had of his brother placed him in that area near where New Mexico, Texas, and Mexico met at a common point. He'd found no sign of Ben before, but he could have missed—

"Don't move, mister!"

The low command came from the brush behind Starbuck. It was the voice of a woman.

TWO

Starbuck froze.

"Put your hands up. Turn around—slow."

Shawn raised his arms, pivoted carefully. A frown knotted his brow. The woman—actually a girl in her late teens, he would guess—looked to be near exhaustion. Her hair, a bright honey-yellow, was tangled and matted, and hung loose about her shoulders. Her eyes seemed to burn, intensifying their blue color, and blood smeared the left side of her face and crusted on the shoulder of the leather jacket she was wearing. Burrs and bits of weeds clung to her rough cloth pants, and in her scratched and bruised hands, she held a sawed-off shotgun of the type used by guards who rode the stagecoaches.

"No need for that," he said quietly, nodding at the twin-muzzled weapon.

"That's for me to say!" the girl snapped, glancing about. "Throw that gun you're carrying over here to me—and no tricks or I'll shoot your head off!"

Starbuck grinned faintly. Reaching down with his right hand, he lifted the pistol from its holster. Carefully holding the butt between a thumb and forefinger, he tossed it at her feet. She was wearing jackboots, he noticed, which were badly scuffed and almost worn through at the toes.

"What's next?" he asked, the smile still twitching the corners of his lips.

The girl, keeping the shotgun trained on him and never removing her eyes from his face, squatted slowly and picked up the pistol.

"I'll tell you what's next," she replied, straightening up and thrusting the pistol under the waistband of her pants, "I'm taking your horse."

Shawn shook his head. "Won't be a good idea."

She considered him coldly. "Why not?"

"He's got no use for strangers."

Her lips pulled down scornfully. "Don't try handing me that hassayampa. A horse is a horse."

Starbuck shrugged. "Suit yourself . . . You in some kind of trouble?"

"Was—not any more since I found something to ride."

"Blood all over you, and you look like you've had rough going. Mind telling me what happened?" Shawn said, allowing his arms to sink slowly.

"Apaches—damn them to hell!" the girl said fervently.

"Around here—close?" he asked, frowning.

"No. Was back up a ways, quite a ways, I guess you could say," she replied, relenting somewhat. "Place they call the Pantano Wash. Was on a stage out of Tucson. We got ambushed—eight of us . . . Back up a bit, mister—against that bush. I want to get to that canteen."

Shawn retreated slowly to the opposite side of the clearing. He watched the girl move to the container of water, pull the cork, and with the shotgun leveled unwaveringly at him, take a long, grateful drink.

"Pantano Wash," he said. "That's about a day's ride southeast of Tucson—"

She nodded, helping herself to more water.

"You the only one that got out alive?"

She hung the canteen back on the stub and replaced the cork. "Far as I know, mister. Only way I managed it was by playing dead. Happened about dark, and while they were stripping the others, I crawled off into the bushes."

"You hurt? All that blood—"

"Come from the man lying next to me. Smeared it on myself to make the Indians think they'd got me, too." She paused, looked toward his saddlebags. "You got something in there to eat?"

"Jerky and biscuits. Didn't cook up anything because of the Apaches. Help yourself to whatever you find."

"You do it for me," the girl said, motioning with the shotgun. "Real careful, now."

Shawn crossed to where the leather pouches lay, dug out the oiled paper in which he'd folded several strips of dried beef. Selecting a large piece, he added a couple of biscuits to it and offered them to her.

She snatched them from his fingers and

motioned again with the barrel of the shotgun. "Now get back over there where I can watch you while I eat."

Starbuck returned to the opposite side of the clearing and dropped to his heels. She shook her head.

"Clear down—flat on your tail. Don't want you getting ideas about jumping me."

Shawn settled on the ground. Higher up on the slope behind them, a ground squirrel squeaked into the lowering light. Instantly, there was a quiet swish of wings as the owl sailed off in the direction of the sound.

The girl ate greedily, hungrily, pausing once or twice to take water. Evidently, she had gone days without either.

"Your folks with you on that stage?" he asked when her hunger at last began to taper off.

"Nope, only me. My mama's dead—been dead since I was twelve. Was on my way to find Pa when the Apaches hit us."

"He around here somewhere?"

"Tombstone—leastwise I've been told he was seen there. And it's where I can expect him to be."

"A prospector—that it?"

"Yeah, been chasing a rainbow ever since I was big enough to know who he was. Place like Tombstone would draw him like sugar draws flies . . . Mind telling me who you are?"

"Starbuck . . . Shawn Starbuck."

"Well, Mr. Starbuck, I'm Glory Cannon. Now, I'm not stealing your horse, I'm only borrowing him so's I can get to Tombstone. I'll leave him at the first livery stable I come to in town and tell the hostler you'll be dropping by to pick him up."

"Heading for there myself," Shawn said, watching her draw herself erect. "Can ride double, go together."

"Like hell we will!" she snapped. "I've lived around men all my life—mining camps and such—and I know just how that'd wind up—with me on the bottom and you on the top somewhere between here and Tombstone! I'll take the horse; you can hoof it. Not far."

"Good twenty-five miles, I expect."

"Won't take a big jack like you but a couple of days to walk that," Glory said, shrugging. She glanced toward the sorrel. Only the gelding's head was visible above the brush. "Saddle still on him?"

"No. Stripped him off for the night."

"Then what we've got to do first off is put your gear back on him. I don't fancy riding all that ways bareback, not when I'm liable to have to make a run for it. Come on, get at it."

"Better forget trying to make it on your own," Shawn warned, not moving. "The sorrel won't let you on his back, for one thing, and between here and Tombstone there's plenty that could happen."

"Not worrying about that!" Glory shot back. "I've been looking out for myself ever since Pa pulled out the last time—six years ago—in a place called Wickenburg."

"Know it some. Worked there for a spell."

"Then you know what I mean. Took care of myself there, can keep right on doing it . . . You going to saddle up that horse, or do I have to rap you over the head with this scattergun to get you in the notion?"

Starbuck got to his feet and started across the small clearing for the deep brush where he had picketed the sorrel. He was watching Glory narrowly, alert for an opportunity to turn, take the shotgun and his pistol away from her. Being stranded afoot, a long way from the settlement, with Apaches known to be lurking in the hills, was the last thing he intended to let happen.

"Better listen to me. That sorrel—"

"Can forget that, Mr. Starbuck! I know a thing or two about horses, same as I do about guns!"

"Hear you tell it, you're mighty smart about a lot of things!"

"A damned sight smarter than you think!" she flared.

In that unguarded moment of anger, Shawn ducked to one side and whirled. His long arms shot out. The fingers of his left hand locked about the barrels of the shotgun, those of the right neatly plucked his pistol from the waistband of her pants, while in the same moment he drove his body into hers, sending her stumbling back into the brush.

She went hard against the springy growth, rocked to one side, righted herself, then faced him, brimming with rage. He nodded, holstered the pistol, and hung the shotgun in the crook of an elbow.

"Now, Miss Glory Cannon," he said, using the same mocking politeness she'd accorded him, "we're going to talk this over."

"Go to hell!" she shouted, and turning, reached for the canteen again.

THREE

Silent, Starbuck watched her take a swallow from the container and then reach into a side pocket of her jacket. Bringing forth a red bandanna handkerchief, she poured a quantity of water onto it and fell to cleaning the blood from her face and neck. That done, she transferred her attention to the leather coat.

"Said you'd lived in Wickenburg for a time," he began.

"Six stinking years—"

"Was there only a short while myself. You know any of the folks at the Skull mine?"

Glory had removed the jacket and was shaking it thoroughly. She wasn't a bad-looking girl, Shawn noted, now that she'd removed the stain from her face and had drawn her hair back into a sort of bun.

"No, we never got that high up. Pa worked at the livery stable after Mama died and before he lit out to find his gold mine. He left me to stay with the Glasgows. He was the man that owned the stable . . . Pa was supposed to send for me."

She draped the jacket over a clump of oak brush and paused to consider him narrowly, as if calculating her chances of recovering the shotgun. Starbuck shook his head, and she turned her attention to the baggy trousers, undoubtedly once owned by her father, that she was wearing.

"You never heard from him, that it?"

"Nope, never wrote or sent word—not once in the whole goddamn six years."

Starbuck grinned. The girl straightened up angrily. "You think that's funny? Well, you just try being a girl in a house where a man's trying to get his hands on you every time his wife's not around—or in a town where you're always having to dodge the drunks and the loafers and the drummers hiding behind every tree!"

"Wasn't what I was thinking about. Was the way you said it."

"What's wrong with how I talk?"

Starbuck shrugged. "Nothing—just a little strong for a girl."

"Woman," she corrected icily. "Got over being a kid a couple of years back. You collecting my fare to Tombstone now or later?"

Shawn considered Glory Cannon thoughtfully. He could not blame her for being cynical; she'd had a rough life so far, one that likely would not improve to any great extent.

"Forget that," he said, and again glanced off into the valley. "I'll get you to Tombstone, and there won't be any charge . . . These Glasgows, they give you the money to leave Wickenburg on?"

The girl was studying him silently, a frown

puckering her brow. At his question, her shoulders stirred.

"Part of it—at least Mrs. Glasgow did. Was glad to get me out of her house, I expect. Saved up the rest from driving rigs around town for the swells and penny-ante poker games. Pa and I used to play a lot in the evenings when he was around. Learned from him."

"Who'd you win the money from?"

"Some of the miners—the ones laid off and not working, or else too old to hold down a regular job. There was the jail-tree, too. Lots of times there'd be prisoners chained to it waiting for the judge. They liked having something to do, and playing poker with me suited them fine."

Starbuck remembered the tree—a big mesquite growing in the center of the settlement, to which malefactors were fastened while they awaited justice, there being no regular jail for such purpose.

"Took me a year to save up enough to buy a ticket to Tucson and have a little left over for the rest of the trip to Tombstone. Dead broke now, however."

"Well, if you can find your pa there, you won't have to worry any—"

"If I find him. Not sure he will be there."

"Probably is. Be the place a man looking for gold or silver would head for soon as the word of a strike got out."

"That why you're going there?"

"No, looking for a man—my brother. Good chance he'll be there."

"Didn't think you looked much like a prospector. More like a cowboy."

"Done a little of everything. Rode shotgun on a bullion wagon when I was in Wickenburg."

Glory Cannon smiled wearily. "You can have Wickenburg far as I'm concerned," she said, and sank onto a small boulder at the fringe of the brush.

Starbuck propped the shotgun against a clump of oak, glanced once more into the valley. Light still lay upon it, but now it was a soft gold, the harshness having gradually vanished as sundown approached.

"That name, Shawn—you part Indian?"

Starbuck shook his head. "My ma was a teacher. Worked among the Indians—the Shawnees. Took my name from them."

"This brother you're looking for have a funny name like that, too?"

"No, his is Benjamin—Ben, we called him. Goes by Damon Friend, too."

"He dodging the law or something?"

"Just a personal thing. He also worked for the Skull outfit in Wickenburg."

The girl stirred. "Don't think I ever heard of him either, but then I wasn't up around the mines much."

A silence fell between them, and then Shawn said, "Told me your pa was a miner. Can't figure why he'd be working in a livery stable in a mining town."

"One damned good reason—John Barleycorn! Pa was a drinker. Couldn't leave the bottle alone, and the mine owners plain wouldn't hire him. Too risky, they said."

Starbuck considered the reply absently. Back deep in his mind, a vague worry that had sprung to life when the girl first appeared now began to grow, take form. He brushed at the stubble on his chin.

"I've been wondering," he said, "is there a chance those Apaches could have missed you at that ambush and set out on your trail?"

"Maybe. I kept looking back after I got away. Never did see any of them."

"Probably wouldn't unless they wanted you to—or didn't care . . . Think about it some; do you know for sure they saw you lying there with the others?"

"Sure. Couple of them came over. One jerked the chain and locket from around my neck. Was Mama's. The other'n started to take my leather jacket, then somebody hollered something at them, and they went over to where one of the men was lying."

Shawn nodded. "Means they know you got away. That brave would have gone back for the jacket. How close to dark was it when they hit you?"

Glory frowned, got to her feet slowly. "I don't exactly remember—I was so scared. About an hour or so, I think, maybe less. Why? Do you think they could've started tracking me?"

"Can bet on it," Starbuck said crisply. "Probably had to stall around till morning before starting, but that wouldn't have made any difference to them."

"Then they could have followed me here—"

"Or be getting close by now. We'd know it if they had caught up . . . Not taking any chances," Shawn added, and crossing the clearing, took up his gear and the shotgun and moved toward the sorrel. "We're getting out of here—fast."

Glory hurriedly pulled on her jacket. Grabbing the canteen and picking up the saddlebags, she fell in behind him.

"Is there any use in running? Won't they just keep on following us?"

"Be dark soon—and we won't leave them much of a trail to—"

He paused. High up on the slope behind them, a coyote barked. Almost immediately, a quavering answer came from a short distance to the north.

"Expect that's them," Starbuck murmured, moving to quickly saddle and bridle the gelding. "Little early for coyotes to be barking. Usually wait until night. Could be the real thing, of course, but we're not about to gamble on it."

Glory half turned, threw a worried glance into the ragged, brushy hills. "Can I do anything?"

Without pausing, Shawn said, "Gather up some dry branches and leaves for a fire. Pile them in the center of the clearing."

"For a fire? Won't that—"

"Draw them? What I'm hoping. We get them to waste some time sneaking up on what they think is our camp, we'll gain a little ground."

At once, the girl turned away and began to assemble a mound of tinder-dry wood and other bits of litter in the open area. By the time Starbuck had finished with the sorrel, she had completed the task.

"Step back there by my horse," he directed, digging into his pocket for a match.

The sound of a coyote echoed across the slopes again, this time coming from below and to the south of them. If it was not Apaches, Shawn thought grimly, then they were being surrounded by the sly little desert dogs.

Striking the match, he tucked it into the base of the woodpile, hesitating long enough to be certain that it had caught. When flames began to lick upward hungrily, he wheeled to the sorrel. Taking a grip on the horse's headstall, he nodded to Glory.

"Mount up—"

She did not protest or hesitate. Grasping the horn in one hand, the cantle in the other, and assisted by Shawn, she went onto the saddle. Hurrying, he swung the gelding about, away from the now crackling fire, and, walking ahead, started down the slope toward the darkening valley.

He kept to the loose rock and thick brush whenever possible, taking pains to leave little evidence of their passage. That he could not hope to fool the Apaches for long was certain; the braves were expert trackers, and while his efforts could make it difficult for them, he was not foolish enough to believe he could elude them for any length of time.

But night was less than an hour away, and if luck was with them, the decoy fire and the effort he was making to conceal their trail could combine to afford an escape.

The broad, sweeping valley lay just ahead. Starbuck altered his course, began to double back northward, careful to stay within the last screening outcrop of brush. He continued on steadily, leading the gelding with the tight-lipped girl crouched on the saddle, at as fast a pace as possible over the loose rock and through the ragged, clinging growth.

Abruptly, a deep wash, breaking off at right angles and leading down into lower ground, appeared. He gave it a moment's consideration:

might as well get off the mountain now. Still holding to the gelding's bridle, he led the horse past the mouth of the arroyo, and then, in a welter of shale and gravel that would not betray their movements, he backtracked to the edge of the wash.

"Hang on," he said tautly, looking up at Glory, and then slapped the sorrel smartly on the hindquarters.

The startled animal leaped forward, sailed down into the bed of the arroyo, then halted, legs quivering. Breaking off a branch from the heart of a nearby rabbitbush, Starbuck quickly brushed out the hoof prints at the top of the wash. That done, he dropped down onto its dry, sandy floor and, following the same procedure with the leafy branch, removed all signs of his and the gelding's presence for a good hundred yards. Satisfied, finally, he threw the bit of brush aside and swung up behind the girl.

"Ought to buy us an hour or so," he said. "I figure that's all we need."

"Are we going to try and make it to Tombstone?" she asked, looking back over her shoulder at him.

"Too far. My horse is tired. He'd never get there carrying double. We'll find another place to camp along the mountain, get an early start in the morning."

Glory's eyes were widening as she looked

beyond him to the mouth of the wash, now a short distance behind and above them.

Starbuck frowned. “What’s the matter?”

The crack of a rifle and the unnerving yell of an Apache was his answer.

FOUR

Starbuck twisted about, swore under his breath. All the precautions he'd taken had gone for naught. One of the Apaches high up on the mountainside had spotted them moving through the brush below. His yell and the report of his rifle would quickly bring the others in his party.

Jamming spurs into the flanks of the tired sorrel, he thrust the reins into Glory's hands.

"Keep close to the bottom of the slope," he said tensely. "I'll try to hold them off until we can find a place to make a stand."

The gelding broke into an uneven lope. Shawn, clamping his legs tight to the horse's barrel body, sought to turn about and be in a position to fire. The first Apache was now down in the wash, crouched low over his pony's outstretched neck as the horse began to lengthen out in pursuit. Beyond him, just reaching the mouth of the arroyo and starting down into it, were four more braves.

Starbuck threw his attention to the land ahead. They were moving along the base of a row of low bluffs. Farther on, he could see where they ended and long slopes once more flowed down from the higher regions and melted into the valley. There was little cover—only short brush, rocks, a few junipers. Jaw set, he looked again to the arroyo.

The lead Apache had reached the end of the wash and was curving into the open. He was beginning to gain on the laboring sorrel. Farther over the rest of the party were strung out in a line as they pounded down the sandy trace toward the valley.

"There's a mine—"

At the girl's voice, Starbuck brought his eyes to the slope along which the gelding rushed. A hundred yards or so up the grade lay the scar of an abandoned shaft—a dark oblong opening in the slate gray of the earth.

"That'll be our only chance," he shouted above the thud of the sorrel's hooves. "Head for it!"

"Your horse—I don't think he can make it!"

"Not with both of us!" Starbuck answered. "When you start climbing, I'll drop off."

She turned to him, face white, strained. "They'll kill you—"

"Maybe not . . . Turn up—here!"

Immediately, Glory veered the gelding onto the slope. The horse slowed instantly and began to labor. Shawn pushed himself backward and slid off the gelding's rump. He hit the uneven ground, staggered, and went to one knee. Righting himself quickly, he wheeled to face the Apache bearing down on him at a gallop. Raising the shotgun, he took quick aim and triggered the left barrel.

The hammer clicked on an empty chamber—or a spent shell. Cursing, Starbuck pulled off the alternate barrel. Again, there was only a dull snap. The weapon had been useless all the time.

Throwing it into the brush, he drew his pistol. The brave, rifle now raised, was leveling the long gun at him as his tan and black pony raced on unguided except for knee pressure. The rifle cracked even as Starbuck faced about. There was a shrill *spang* as the bullet struck a rock on the slope behind him and ricocheted noisily off into space.

Starbuck backed slowly up the slope in the wake of Glory and the sorrel. Pistol steadied on his right forearm, he waited coolly for the Apache to get in handgun range. The brave, levering another cartridge into the chamber of his rifle, fired again. The bullet went far wide. At that moment, Shawn squeezed off his shot. The Apache rocked to one side, clawed at the mane of his horse, and then fell heavily to the ground, still clinging to his weapon with one hand.

The remaining braves began to open up. Bullets dug into the slope below Starbuck, falling short. They would be within range quickly, however, and unless he could reach the old mine, find cover in the piles of rotting timbers or in the shaft, he'd have little chance to—

Rifle shots crackled from the slope above him. Starbuck glanced up. Glory had reached the small plateau fronting the mine and was dropping off the sorrel. A second figure, that of a man, was kneeling at the rim of the flat, long-barreled weapon pointing down at the Indians.

The Apaches had slowed, were pulling to a stop, uncertain of the wisdom of moving closer in the face of the rifleman stationed on the hillside. Starbuck waited no longer. He was within range of the braves, and it would be foolhardy to tempt them. Holstering his weapon, he began to climb the slope in long, plunging steps.

Again, the Indians brought their weapons into play, which, in turn, got an instant response from the plateau. Shawn could hear the *thunk* of bullets driving into the hard soil around him, felt one pluck at his sleeve as he rushed on.

He gained the flat gasping for breath, the muscles of his legs screaming in pain from the climb. Glory ran forward to meet him, a smile of relief on her face. Brushing at the sweat misting his eyes, he rested himself against a sagging remnant of a wooden trestle.

"Was a close one—"

She nodded as he looked back down into the valley. The Apaches had retrieved their dead member and were heading toward the wash. Starbuck shifted his attention to the man at the rim of the plateau, now on his feet and moving up to meet him.

He was a short, stocky individual, and wore a

coarse shirt, leather vest, and heavy shoes instead of the usual boots preferred by most prospectors. The slack legs of his woolen pants had been gathered about the ankles and calves and secured in legging fashion with rawhide cord.

He had watery blue eyes, a splotched, ruddy face framed by white hair, and a beard that showed considerable tobacco staining.

"Howdy, folks, I'm Pete Lusky," he said, extending a work-scarred hand. "Right pleased to see you ain't been nicked."

"Thanks to you," Starbuck replied, and introduced Glory and himself. "Plenty glad you happened to be up here."

Lusky glanced at the departing Indians and wagged his head. "Them danged savages—man just ain't safe nowheres around here with them running loose!"

Beyond the old prospector, Shawn could see a gray and white burro dozing near a thin juniper. The sorrel, legs spread, head down, flanks still heaving, was close by.

"You working this mine?" Shawn asked, pulling away from the weathered timbers.

Pete Lusky shook his head. "Naw, just aimed to camp here for the night. Diggings belonged to Artie Jay. Weren't nothing here, so he give it up, moved on . . . You folks heading for Tombstone?"

"Figured to in the morning. Apaches showed up, and we had to break camp, run for it."

"Was in Tombstone myself a week or so back. Sure is something! What're you planning on doing now?"

Starbuck glanced at Glory. She was leaning against the framework entrance to the shaft, regarding him intently.

"Like to put up here for the night if it's all right with you."

"I'll be real obliged to you if you will!" Lusky said heartily. "Jackass of mine sure ain't much company—and I got me a pot of beans and salt pork ready to warm up, and was about to stir up some chicory when I heard the shooting. You're welcome to set in on eating with me."

"Be a pleasure," Shawn said, "but we don't want to work on your grub. Got a little of our own left—"

"Pshaw! I eat till I run out, then I finagle some more somewheres. Ain't no big thing, this eating . . . Now, you and the lady just set down there on that log, and I'll start things to going. Won't take no more'n a minute or two, then we can chow . . . And don't worry none about them blasted redskins. They won't be coming back—leastwise not tonight. You're safe up here as you'd be in church—unless you get too close to that danged jackass of mine. Meanest goddamn critter—excuse me, missus—on this green earth! I'm telling you that for sure!"

Shawn glanced at Glory Cannon and winked.

Pete Lusky was a talking man, there was no doubt of that. The girl smiled back, and moving on by her, he began to strip his gear from the sorrel. The big gelding was dead beat, but a night's rest would put him back in good shape. He could use some sleep, too, he realized, and he reckoned that went for Glory as well.

FIVE

"You ever run into a prospector named Ira Cannon?"

Glory asked the question of Pete Lusky after their meal was finished and they were sitting by the fire drinking the last of the bitter chicory the old miner had brewed.

"Cannon?" Lusky repeated, clawing at his beard. "Seems I do recollect the name, but can't rightly say where or why . . . They's so danged many folks traipsing around through these hills nowadays that a man just can't keep up with who's coming or going. He some kin of your'n?"

"My pa. Heard he'd been seen in Tombstone."

Lusky wagged his head. "Who ain't? That there place is like an ant hill, people a-swarming all over it. I'm betting there's a thousand galoots living in tents there on Goose Flat, besides them that's in the town itself!

"And that town—it's a reg'lar city! Got maybe forty or fifty buildings going up—some of them just about done. Expect there's maybe a couple hundred folks living there—and streets, why, they got them all marked out and named. Calling the main one Allen."

"Have you spent much time there?" Shawn asked.

"Some. Dang place is just too rich for my blood. Plain can't afford them prices."

"I'm looking for somebody, too," Starbuck continued, and made his inquiry concerning Ben.

Again, the prospector stroked thoughtfully at his beard. Finally, "Nope, don't think I ever heard the name, excepting from you. Not the other'n you say he's using, either."

Starbuck's thick shoulders stirred slightly. Long ago, he'd become accustomed to failure insofar as his quest for his brother was concerned. In the beginning, as a raw farm boy fresh from Ohio, his first disappointment had come when he learned Ben was not where he had been positive he would be. The revelation had filled him with despair, but he had continued the search, patiently investigating every rumor and checking each report, during which time the sharp edge of failure gradually grew duller until now, some five years since the day on which he had set forth, rebuff was ordinary, the accepted norm. But frustrating as it was, there was no lessening of his stubborn determination to find Ben.

"Tombstone," Glory murmured, "how'd they ever come to pick a name like that for the town?"

Pete Lusky, obviously enjoying himself, leaned back against a rock and drew a pipe and an oil-skin pouch from his coat pocket. The night had chilled since sundown, and Starbuck had taken a blanket from his roll and draped it around the girl's shoulders. For his own comfort, he had donned his brush jacket.

"Wasn't no they, was a him," Lusky said, stuffing the charred bowl of the briar with shreds of tobacco. "Name was Schieffelin—Ed Schieffelin. Prospector like myself and a couple hundred others—always looking for a bonanza. Took it in his head to do some digging in these here hills one day."

Pete hesitated, plucked a burning brand from the fire, held it to the pipe, and puffed it into life.

"He run into a old friend about that time. Was a scout for the Army, somebody said. Asked Ed where he was lining out for, and when Ed told him, he said, "You ain't going to find nothing in them San Pedro hills but your tombstone. Apaches'll lift your hair, for sure."

"Well, Ed, being a hardheaded Dutchman, didn't pay him no mind, just went right on about his business. Didn't turn up much at first, but before it was over, he'd staked out a mine he called the Lucky Cuss—and it sure was because the ore that come out of it assayed better'n fifteen thousand dollars a ton!

"Then he found another'n he named the Tough Nut Lode, and another'n he called the Contention because there was some kind of argument over it. Lost out on the one folks call the Grand Central. Seems he had to go chasing after his jackass when it got loose, and while he was gone some other fellows stumbled onto it. If it hadn't been for that blamed jackass, I reckon the Grand Central would've been his, too—not that he needed it. Got hisself a couple a dozen barrels of money from them others."

"He still around?" Starbuck asked.

"Yeah, reckon he is. Ain't seen him lately, but I've heard him spoke of. Like I said, I don't hang around that town, and he ain't got the time to prospect no more, so we just don't bump into each other like once we did."

"Can see why everybody across the country's heading for Tombstone," Shawn said. "Mines rich as those you've mentioned are bound to draw a crowd . . . The silver hard to get out?"

Far off to the south, a gunshot flatted hollowly through the star-stuck night. Lusky considered the lonely sound thoughtfully for a long moment, stirred.

"Well, all depends on where a man's digging. Sometimes a fellow runs across a ledge sticking right out of the ground. Ain't no chore at all then. Was the kind of luck Ed Schieffelin had. Come onto a ledge of ore so dang pure he could press a quarter into it and read the date. Then there's the kind a man's got to go down deep for. It's just like everything else in life, I reckon—all a matter of luck."

"You ever hit it big?"

"Me? Nope, piddlin' stuff mostly. Had me

a claim north of here I was working. Assayed about two thousand to the ton. Then it went and pinched out on me about the time I got to where it was paying . . . Didn't much care. Don't know what I'd do was I ever to get a pile of money like Ed Schieffelin. Be plumb lost if I wasn't out in these here hills a-dodging redskins and cussing that jackass. Sort of gets inside a man, that kind of living, and it don't ever turn him loose.

"Heard from somebody that Schieffelin was feeling sort of that way—was even thinking about going somewheres, California or maybe it was up Oregon way, and doing some prospecting for gold. The hunting and the digging gets in a man's blood, sort of turns him upside down so's nothing else ever counts for much."

Shawn cast a glance at Glory. She was staring into the fire, her features stilled. Pete Lusky was telling her nothing she did not know; her awareness of the thirst that besets some men and drives them relentlessly on in a search for riches was firsthand.

She was thinking of her father in those moments, he guessed, and the task of finding him in the booming settlement of Tombstone where he reportedly had been seen. That Glory Cannon was capable of taking care of herself had been proved, but she would need help.

"You happen to know if the law in Tombstone is a man named Earp? Figured to ask him about—"

"Law!" the prospector hooted. "There ain't no such thing! Closest one's the sheriff in Tucson. He's been going to send down a deputy to try and keep things straight, but he just ain't never got around to it . . . There just ain't nothing like that yet—no gov'ment, not even any vigilantes, that's how wild things is. Oh, they's some fellows getting together, I hear tell, that's aiming to set up some kind of a city gov'ment—mayor and councilmen, things like that, and they're figuring to hire on a town marshal once they get organized and can find a man fool enough to take on the job, but until they do, things are going every which-a-way.

"The town's wilder'n a bunch of Mexican goats! Why, there ain't a single day goes by that somebody don't get killed and lugged off to Boot Hill . . . Who's this here Earp you're talking about?"

"Lawman I met up in Kansas—Dodge City. Was told there that he'd moved to Tombstone. Figured he'd probably be wearing a badge there by now."

Lusky knocked the dottle from his pipe and refilled it. "Expect he'd be mighty welcome to it, if that's what he wants—whether they got a town gov'ment or not. He pretty good?"

"One of the best—"

"That's what it'll take," the prospector said, relighting his briar. "Man'll have to be tough and mean and ready to use his gun, and if he's that kind, I'm hoping he will show up. Tombstone could be a fine little town if somebody'd just sail in there and settle them high-binders and slickers down . . . It real important you find him?"

"Mainly wanted to ask him about Glory's pa and my brother. A marshal or a sheriff is usually the best place to get information. Since there's not either one, we'll have to try something else."

The girl looked up quickly, eyes on Starbuck.

"Ain't but one way I can see," Lusky said. "Just start asking everybody you run into. Luck'll probably be better was you to start with them that's camped outside town. They're the ones traipsing the hills every day. Like as not somebody'll have come across her pa."

"Ought to be a quicker way," Shawn murmured, and feeling Glory's eyes pushing against him, looked at her questioningly. "I say something wrong?"

She smiled, shook her head. "No, nothing like that. It was what you said—that we would be looking for my pa. Did you mean it that way—the both of us together?"

Starbuck frowned. "Sure—if you want it that way."

The girl settled back, gaze once again dreamy and lost in the dwindling flames of the fire. "I do," she said quietly.

Shawn pulled himself to his feet, crossed the

clearing to a pile of broken timbers. Selecting a couple, he returned, added them to the fire.

"Ought to keep it going for the night," he said, and looked down at the girl. "Expect we'd best be getting some sleep. Tomorrow'll be a hard day—and it'll begin early."

"Reckon that goes for me, too," Lusky said, also rising. "But before it slips my mind, I want to say one thing—this sure has been a pleasurable evening. I want to thank you folks for it."

"We're obliged to you," Starbuck said, reaching a hand to Glory and helping her up. "Just hope we can run into each other again someday . . . Good night."

"Same here," the old prospector said, moving off toward his bedroll. "Good night."

SIX

It was still the half-light of pre-dawn when they left the abandoned mine and headed down the slope for the valley below. Shawn, in the saddle of the sorrel with Glory Cannon riding behind him, was anxious to get an early start and be well on the way to Tombstone before the day wore on too far.

Pete Lusky, however, was in no hurry—possibly because he led a life that followed no timetable, or it could have been because the long-eared burro that he called only by the name of Critter was at best a reluctant partner with a will of his own.

Their relationship appeared to be one of continual warfare, which began in the morning when Lusky sought to make ready the stubborn little animal and ended at dark when he endeavored to remove the pack. The interim hours were filled with a constant nipping with sharp teeth and a lashing out of hooves on the part of Critter, countered by a prolonged cursing, slapping, kicking, and cudgeling on the part of the old prospector.

The day had begun shortly after the meal was over, with Lusky's efforts to load the wooden saddle—a feat accomplished only after the jack had done much pitching and bucking and made several attempts to bite his owner. In turn he had been the recipient of a number of hard blows on the nose and across the ears from the short length of fence post Lusky carried as a club. Later, as they descended the hillside, the burro twice crowded the old man off the trail, once knocking him to his knees.

But it all transpired in an air of everyday routine which, as they moved into the valley, prompted Starbuck to shake his head wonderingly at Lusky.

"This go on all the time?"

The prospector looked at him blankly as if not understanding and then nodded. "Oh, you're meaning the way me and Critter gets along. Yeah, reckon you could say so. Ain't no harm done. Just have to keep showing that danged jughead who's the boss . . . Well, I'll be leaving you here."

"You're not going to Tombstone?"

"Nope, was there a while back, ain't no cause to go there again. Got my eyes on some hills a ways on north. Something tells me I'll make a strike there."

Shawn nodded. "Hope you do . . . Obliged to you for your hospitality, and good luck."

"Hospitality ain't nothing but good manners, and you're mighty welcome. So long and good luck to you both."

Lusky turned away at once, smacking Critter

alongside the head with his club to get him pointed in the right direction, delivering another to the hindquarters to start him forward. The burro responded with a savage nip at the prospector's thigh and then moved out.

"Pete reminds me of Pa, somehow," Glory said as Starbuck put the sorrel into a lope. "Not the way he looks so much, but how he talks—never gives up thinking about the strike he's going to make someday."

"Men like him live on the future," Shawn agreed. "Whether they ever find what they're looking for doesn't always seem to matter."

They became aware of Tombstone long before they reached the settlement. A thick pall of dirty gray became visible shortly after they rode out of the short hills, and then they heard a low droning sound which grew increasingly louder as they approached. Not long after, they entered an area densely packed with tents and makeshift shelters, among which men in boots and coarse clothing, and slatternly women, moved about busily. But the confusion they encountered there fell far short of what greeted them in the settlement itself.

The dust in the street, a whitish lime film, was inches deep, and was constantly stirred into drifting clouds by a milling horde of people, by the burros, horses, and lumber-laden wagons arriving from the nearby Chiricahua and Huachuca mountains. Huge ore wagons drawn by a dozen or more mules, buggies and coaches, and men on horseback contributed to creating a choking, blinding fog that no one appeared to notice.

Construction was under way at every hand, and the pound of hammers and rip of saws made a continuous racket that mixed with voices shouting back and forth, the din of traffic, and an occasional gunshot. Allen Street, so designated by a sign placed high on a post, was lined with shacks, a few fairly good wooden buildings, and many were a combination of horizontally laid boards and canvas. Saloons, gambling casinos, dance halls, and restaurants were everywhere, all without name other than a word or two detailing their reason for existence.

Prospectors, mining men in corduroy and laced boots, swaggering cowhands, frock-coated gamblers, extravagantly dressed women, drummers, and tight-faced businessmen all flowed along the teeming roadway in a ceaseless stream.

Starbuck, pulling back out of the rush at a corner where a side street made its intersection, considered the crush moodily.

"Finding anybody in this town will be more than just a big job," he said. "Going to have to come up with a better idea than just asking everybody we see."

Two heavily armed men emerged from the

alleyway behind them, strolled by, both giving Glory close attention before they disappeared into Allen Street's swirl.

"What else can we do?"

Starbuck wiped at the dust settling on his face. "Was thinking that prospectors come in to have the ore they've dug assayed, see if their claim's worth anything. Be my guess your pa will have done that if he's here and working the hills anywhere close."

Glory nodded. "He's around here—and he'll be prospecting."

"Thing to do then is hunt up the assayers, talk to them," Shawn said, wheeling the sorrel about. "Saw a livery stable down the street when we came in. I'll leave my horse there."

Breasting the traffic, all moving toward the center of the settlement, Shawn doubled back to where the stable, no more than a roof over a series of narrow partitions, had been erected. Leaving the gelding with the hostler, a young Mexican, and instructing him to give the horse a ration of grain and all the hay and water he wanted, Starbuck swung into the flow, holding firmly to the girl's arm.

Several times en route he pushed aside men who crowded in close, smiling in friendly fashion and with question in their eyes, but it came to no more than that, and finally they found themselves in the heart of the town—and with no idea at all as to where in the midst of such disorder an assay office might be found.

Shawn, spotting a fairly well-dressed man with papers bulging his pocket, halted him as he threaded a course through the throng.

"Looking for an assayer. You tell me where we can find one?"

The man bobbed, studied him closely. "You got a claim you're working? I'm a lawyer—can help you with the legal end of—"

"Nothing like that. Trying to locate a prospector named Ira Cannon. Figured the easiest way to do it would be through an assayer."

"Probably will be at that," the lawyer said. "You'll find most of them on a side street down a piece—first corner to your left . . . Now, if you need some legal advice, my name's Willborn. Find me here in front of this saloon most anytime—leastwise you will until I can get an office built."

"Obliged," Starbuck said, and taking Glory's arm again, moved on.

The quarters of the first assayer, a square of head-high, rough-surfaced boards roofed over with canvas, was crowded. When it came his turn, Shawn made the inquiry, was told Ira Cannon was a name unknown, and to try the next office.

With the girl in tow, he did, again met failure, and headed for the third establishment. There the assayer, John Trimm, a tall, ruddy-faced man with reddish hair and a quick, nervous way about him, nodded his head.

"Who's asking?"

"Name's Starbuck. You know him?"

"Sure I do. What about it?"

SEVEN

Starbuck heaved a quiet sigh. It had taken less time and effort than he'd anticipated. Feeling Glory press against him, he moved aside, allowed her to step forward.

"Is he around somewhere?" she asked.

Trimm frowned, considered her narrowly. "You got some business with Ira Cannon?"

"I'm his daughter," she replied.

The assayer's brows lifted in surprise. Several other men gathered in the crudely built office ceased their talking and swung their attention to the girl.

Starbuck, aware of the abrupt hush, swept them with his glance, nodded to Trimm.

"Answer the lady's question," he directed in a cool voice.

"Sure, sure," the assay man said hurriedly. "Just wasn't expecting him to have any kin."

"Where can we find him?"

"Out at his claim, I expect, putting it in shape to work."

"Then he's made a strike?"

"Yeah, sure has," Trimm said, his manner now more cordial. "Don't know exactly how good it is. First assays were fair."

Conversation between the bystanders, now that

their curiosity had been appeased, had resumed. Two of them took their leave.

"How do we get to his claim?" Shawn asked.

"It's about five miles up the valley. Go back down Allen Street, take the road out of town. Mine will be on your left. Calls it the Glory."

Shawn glanced at the girl. She was looking down, and while he could not see her eyes, he suspected there were tears in them. She was not nearly as tough as she made out to be.

"Would that be your name?" Trimm wondered.

The girl nodded.

"Well, you won't have any trouble locating him. If you get lost, ask the first man you bump into where you can find Ira Cannon. Like as not he'll know."

Starbuck said, "Obliged," and dropping an arm around Glory's shoulders, returned to the bustling street.

"I guess Pa's happy now," she said as they turned into the traffic and moved toward the livery stable. "He's finally got himself a mine."

"Aren't you?"

Her lips pulled into a small smile. "I guess so. I just hope it's worth something—and that he'll hang onto it."

"From the way Trimm and the others back there acted, it must be a pretty good claim . . . And as far as seeing that he doesn't lose it—that's something you can do a lot about."

"Pretty hard to fight a bottle of whiskey," Glory said in a falling voice. "I saw my mother go to her grave trying to do that. I'm not sure I'm even as strong as she was."

"Could be you're overlooking something," Shawn said as they fought their way through the crowd. "Whiskey was probably a crutch for him, something to keep him going because he felt he was a failure. Now that he's found what he always wanted, he won't be needing a crutch."

He felt her fingers tighten about his wrist. "Do you really think it could be that way?"

"Worked out like that plenty of times before, no reason why it'll be any different with him—anyway, we'll soon know," Starbuck answered as they turned into the makeshift livery barn.

They rode out of town at a fair lope, Glory again behind him on the saddle. The sorrel, better for the two hours or so in the stable, where he'd taken his fill of feed, was anxious to run, but traffic was only a little less congested in the outskirts of the settlement, and they covered a good quarter mile before the horse could have his way.

As they struck off through the hills, the country gradually grew rougher, with rock ledges thrusting out of the dark soil here and there and piles of weather-smoothed boulders barring their way occasionally. Vegetation was scant—mostly a short brown grass that showed fire scar and weed clumps that bore evidence of much trampling. Glory, her gaze anxiously sweeping the slopes as they progressed up the valley, began to betray her nervousness.

"Shawn—could we have taken the wrong road?"

He shook his head. "Only one out of town. We're still a mile or so short of five."

The land continued to become more ragged, with rock formations increasingly plentiful and the slopes much steeper. They encountered no one on the road, but there were signs of prospecting being done or having been attempted on the sides of every hill. The unmistakable thump of a pick being wielded came to them regularly, and once they heard the dull boom of an explosion as someone beyond the line of bluffs set off a charge of powder.

"Should be getting close," Starbuck said, pulling the gelding to a halt and scanning the surrounding country closely. "Might save time if we'd—"

"There—up that draw!" Glory said suddenly, pointing. "I can see something—a mine shaft, maybe . . . And there's a sign over it."

Shawn followed the line of her leveled finger. They had overridden a small canyon on their left, and shading his eyes with a hand, he made out a diggings at its upper end and well above the floor of the valley.

"Could be it," he said, and pulling the sorrel

about, sent him loping for the narrow gash in the slope.

They reached the mouth of the canyon and again halted. Brush now hid the flat where the shaft had been dug into the wall of the arroyo, but the trail leading up to it was plain and showed considerable travel.

Starbuck raked the gelding with his spurs and started him up the grade. A few stunted junipers studded the nearby slopes, and camp-robber jays, with bright, beady eyes peering out from their black masks, darted about in the brush scolding angrily.

The sorrel broke out onto a small plateau littered with boxes, cans, bits of lumber, and mining tools. A solitary burro in a pen at the opposite side raised its elongated head and considered them indifferently. Starbuck pointed to the sign above the shaft's entrance. The name GLORY had been etched with charcoal on the rough surface of a bit of discarded shoring.

At once, the girl slipped from her place behind him and dropped to the ground. She remained there, motionless, seemingly reluctant to go any farther, as if fearful of once again coming face to face with her long-missing parent.

The camp was unusually quiet. Giving that thought, Starbuck swung off the gelding. Since Cannon's burro was there, it seemed unlikely the man would be away.

“Where is he?” Glory asked, turning to face Shawn. “I don’t hear any digging—”

Starbuck tied the horse to a clump of oak and, stepping up to the girl’s side, cupped his hands about his mouth.

“Ira Cannon!” he shouted.

There was no response. The prospector could be somewhere up on the slope, beyond earshot, cutting timber that grew well back from the valley. Too, he could be further exploring his claim.

“Cannon!” Starbuck called again in a louder voice.

The name echoed softly along the slopes but brought no answering hail.

“Could he have been in Tombstone—maybe getting supplies?” Glory wondered.

Shawn pointed to the burro. “He would have taken him along to carry back the load.”

“Then where is he?”

Starbuck, apprehension now building within him, dropped his hand to the pistol at his side and moved toward the dark rectangle that was the shaft’s entrance. He had gotten the impression from John Trimm that Cannon had just located his claim, had yet to start working it. If true, the shaft would be little more than an opening and of no depth. If the man was inside, he should have heard the summons easily.

Shawn drew up suddenly. In that same instant,

a gasp slipped from Glory's lips. Lying just inside the shaft was a man. His eyes were wide in death as they stared unseeingly back at them.

"That's Pa," Glory said in an emotionless voice.

EIGHT

Starbuck threw his glance about. They appeared to be alone, and stepping forward, he hunched beside the body of the prospector. His fingers went to the man's throat, probed for the spark of life he knew wasn't there. Cannon's skin was cold, firm; he had been dead for a day or more, victim of a bullet. The chest wound showed no powder burns. Likely, the killer had been standing off at a distance in the brush.

Glory knelt beside him, her eyes on the bearded face of her father. For a long minute, she studied the slack features, and then murmured, "Poor Pa, always a loser. I guess it just wasn't to be for him . . . You think it was the Apaches?"

The girl was amazingly calm, almost undisturbed, but Shawn supposed that was to be expected. She had neither seen nor heard from her parent in years. He would be almost a stranger.

"Doubt it. Apaches would have raided the camp, taken everything that caught their eyes. Rifle's still here," he added, pointing to the weapon leaning against a wall of the shallow excavation. "Sure wouldn't have left it."

"Then who—"

Starbuck got to his feet, moved to Cannon's bedroll. Jerking one of the blankets free, he dropped back and spread it over the lifeless body.

"Anybody's guess," he said as the girl rose and drew aside. "Could be some claim jumper, but I hardly think so. Wasn't robbery. Tools and gear would be gone if—"

He broke off, turned toward the trail. A rattle of gravel had come to him, warning of someone's approach.

"Over here," he said in a low whisper, and taking Glory by the arm, crossed quickly to the opposite edge of the flat.

Silent, they waited out the long moments. The noise on the trail grew louder—the clatter of loose shale, the crack and swish of brush, the chiding of jays protesting the passage of another interloper. Shortly, a bearded figure, one step behind his burro, moved into view. Tension drained from Starbuck. It was Pete Lusky.

"Howdy, again!" he called cheerfully, waving. "Was coming across the hill when I seen you folks heading into this draw. Figured you'd found the lady's Pa and told myself I ought to stop and shake hands."

Starbuck, with Glory at his side, walked slowly back to the center of the clearing where the older man had halted.

A frown crossed Lusky's face. "Something wrong here?"

Shawn pointed to the shaft. "Cannon. He's been shot—killed."

The prospector swore softly, pulled off his hat.

"I'm sure sorry to hear that," he said, running fingers through his thin hair. "Been a lot of that going on around here."

Stepping up to Cannon's body, he drew back the blanket and studied the man's features. "Nope, ain't never seen him before, but like I said, there's so many folks in this country nowadays, just don't hardly ever seen anybody you know . . . You got any idea who might've done it? Can see it weren't the Indians," he finished, replacing the blanket and rising.

Starbuck shrugged. "About all we can tell is that it was somebody standing off in the brush. Probably was using a rifle."

Lusky mumbled his agreement and turned to Glory. "Said I was real sorry, missy, and I mean it. This is a mighty bad thing for you."

Glory nodded woodenly. There was still no sign of tears, and likely there would be none.

"What are you aiming to do about it?" the miner said, coming back to Shawn.

"Not sure. No point in going into Tombstone and reporting it. There's nobody to report it to if there's no lawman."

"You're right there—and killings are about as common as hairs on a dog. Could do some asking around, see if there was somebody had it in for the missy's pa. Then if you found who it was, you could settle with him yourself or haul him up to the sheriff in Tucson."

"Murder is something I don't like to see passed up," Starbuck said. "Ought to try and run down whoever it was that did it." He paused, glanced at Glory. "What do you think about it?"

The girl gave it thought. Then, "I don't see what we can do. Like as not we'd never find out who it was, and if we did it wouldn't help Pa any."

"It's murder," Starbuck said. "Not right to just forget it. Was somebody with a grudge, I'd guess. Why else would they kill him? Nothing worth stealing and the mine's hardly started."

"Wouldn't make no difference to some of these jacklegs hanging around here. Man working a claim gets hisself killed, makes room for somebody else to take it over. Ain't nothing but miner's law in this country, and it ain't going to pay no attention to that kind of goings-on unless the dead man had a partner who'd step up and take over . . . You reckon he had a partner?"

"Don't know," Starbuck replied thoughtfully. "Could probably find out from Trimm."

"Trimm? Who's he?"

"Assayer we talked to in town. Cannon's had dealings with him, it seems. Was Trimm who told us where we could find him."

Lusky clawed at his beard. "Don't recollect him. Fellow I go to's named Campbell."

"Well, partner or not, what Cannon owned now belongs to Glory—"

"What I was thinking," the old prospector said quietly, "and if it's some jasper looking to take over the claim now that he's got him out of the way—you'd best keep a sharp eye on the missy, because if he's wanting it that bad, he'll be after her soon as he finds out she's took over the claim . . . That assayer say Cannon's ore was good?"

"Seemed to think it showed promise," Shawn answered. "Something about it assaying fair."

"Like most of the claims being worked, I reckon. Schieffelin and a couple others that got here first found the real rich stuff. Still, I expect this here claim's worth something."

"Apparently worth killing for," Starbuck murmured. "Belongs to Glory now, so it's up to her what happens next."

Lusky faced the girl standing before him, back turned to the valley. "If you aim to work it, I'll be mighty pleased to hang around, see you get started right. Can hire yourself a couple of Mex' laborers to do the hard work, make some kind of an arrangement to get your ore hauled to the stamp mill at Charleston."

"Where's that from here?"

"Down the river, ten-twelve mile—"

Glory shrugged wearily. "I haven't any money to do anything with."

Pete Lusky cocked his head to one side, scratched at his jaw. "Sort of makes it another kind of mule. You'll have to get grub for the help, and there'll be supplies you'll be needing. Can probably stall paying wages until you get your first load to the mill—but that'd be sort of a gamble. Might not be worth much . . . Just about flat broke myself or I'd be willing to pitch in."

"Goes for me, too," Starbuck said. "Down to my last eagle. If it'll do you any good, you're welcome to it. Can count me in on lending a hand right along with Pete—not that I know anything about mining."

Glory smiled. "Thank you both, but I couldn't let you do it. I'll have to think of something else, or just give up on it . . . Might be the thing to do since I don't know if the claim's worth anything or not."

"Somebody thinks it is," Shawn said.

"And you ain't never going to know unless you work it," Lusky added.

Glory looked off in the direction of Tombstone. "Maybe I could find someone in town who'd be willing to back me."

Lusky bobbed. "Well, they's a plenty of them capitalist fellows around, but they're looking for a sure thing. They'd want to know how good your claim is before they'd sink any cash into it. You don't catch them taking no chances—and I reckon that puts us right back where we started."

"Maybe, but it's still the only answer," Starbuck said. "Trimm's the key. We get a statement from him showing what the ore is worth a ton. If it's good, then you've got something to back up your asking for a loan."

"That's the ticket!" Lusky said approvingly. "Be smart to dig out some new samples, take them in to that fellow Trimm for another look. Can go by what your pa hauled in the first time, and what you're into now, then sort of average what the ore'll bring. Deal like that ought to satisfy any of them money-grabbers."

Shawn looked at the girl. Her features had come alive as they talked, and now there was a brightness in her eyes as plans for her continuing the operation of the mine took shape.

"If only I could—"

"Why not?" Lusky demanded. "If the claim's a good one, you won't have no trouble finding a backer or getting a partner if you want one."

Glory smiled at the old prospector and then at Starbuck. "Would—would you two be interested in—"

"Can count me in," Lusky said quickly.

Shawn's shoulders moved slightly. "Far as getting things started, you can count me in, too, but not as a partner. Brother I spoke of—I've got to find him before I can settle down . . . Appreciate the offer, however."

Glory lowered her eyes and nodded dispiritedly. "Was just a thought," she murmured, and then bent down. "Why this looks like Pa's lucky coin!" she continued, fingers reaching for a dully shining disk half buried in the loose soil.

In that same instant, a gunshot crackled flatly from the slope outside. Pete Lusky stiffened. A puzzled look crossed his grizzled features as a red stain began to spread across his chest.

"Hell—I been shot," he muttered, and slowly sank to the ground.

NINE

The echoes were still rolling as Starbuck threw himself at the girl and carried her down with him.

"Don't move!" he said hoarsely, drawing his pistol.

Crawling to the edge of the flat, he raised his head cautiously and began a thorough search of the distant hillside. Whoever had fired the shot intended for Glory, he was certain—was hiding in the maze of rocks and brush.

He could see no sign, no bit of color or slight movement that would indicate the location of the bushwhacker. Taut with anger, Shawn shifted his attention to the girl, lying prone on the ground where he had left her. She could still be in danger. If the killer, realizing his bullet had found the wrong target, sought a second chance, he needed only to climb higher on the slope to get the girl in his sights again.

"Crawl into the mine shaft," he yelled. "Keep low and don't show yourself."

Glory, her face chalky white, nodded and began to worm her way toward the opening in the hill. Starbuck waited until she had disappeared into the dark cavity, and then, working backward, and flat on his belly, he gained a pile of boulders at the lower end of the plateau. Still keeping his eyes on the gray-green slope across the canyon, he dropped to the brush a dozen feet below the rim of the clearing.

Landing on the slanting, uneven ground, he staggered, went to one knee. Recovering his balance instantly, he hunched, then began to circle toward where he believed the hidden marksman would be. There had not been any betraying sound or motion that would give him an idea of exactly where the killer waited, but he had the general location fixed in his mind, and he kept his gaze locked on that area.

Reaching a small cross draw about halfway down the hillside, he halted. Crouched behind a clump of oak, Starbuck again carefully probed the tangled mass of brush and rock, now no more than fifty yards distant . . . nothing . . . The killer was either lying low or else had pulled back and was climbing to a higher position on the slope, where he would have the mine and the clearing fronting it under his gun.

Shawn turned his thoughts to the ground immediately before him. By staying low, he could cross the arroyo, reach the opposing slope, and work his way to its summit. By so doing, he would break out somewhere between the mine and anyone attempting to get a line on the clearing and a ridge of rocks he could see, and that, logically, would be the point for which the killer would be moving.

Starbuck drew himself upright, swore deeply. From the valley below, and beyond the hill before him, the quick tattoo of a fast-running horse came to him. The killer had chosen not to make a second try for Glory Cannon's life, had instead cut back to where he had left his mount and was now riding for Tombstone at a hard gallop.

Angling across to the trail, Shawn returned to the trail and climbed back to the plateau. Glory, heeding his order, was still inside the shaft. As he stepped into view, she came out at once. Her features no longer showed fear, and her eyes now flickered with anger.

"That bullet was meant for me, wasn't it?"

Starbuck nodded as he hurried toward Lusky. The old miner could still be alive. "Worst part of it is that he got away. Never had a look at him."

He reached the prospector, knelt beside him. Death had been almost instantaneous, he guessed; the bullet had driven into his chest near center.

"It was the same man that killed Pa, wasn't it?"

Rising, Shawn took another of the blankets from Ira Cannon's bedroll and covered Pete Lusky. "Stands to reason."

Baffled, Glory shook her head. "How could it be? Nobody around this place knows I'm here—or even who I am!"

"Not true anymore," Starbuck said, again probing the slope. "Was a dozen men hanging around Trimm's office while we were there. They all heard you tell him who you are. Killer could be one of them . . . I've got a hunch this claim of your pa's is worth a lot more than we think."

"And there's somebody wanting it so bad he's killed Pa and now is trying to kill me?"

"That's the way I see it."

Glory looked down at Lusky's draped figure. "Poor Pete—he'd be alive if I hadn't stooped down to pick up that lucky piece Pa always carried . . . I'm sorry it happened that way."

Starbuck continued to stare out over the valley. Shadows were beginning to lengthen, and the thought of making the long ride back to Tombstone with darkness closing in did not appeal to him. The killer could be expecting them to do just that and be waiting in ambush.

"Expect we'd best spend the night here," he said. "Can fix you a bed inside the shaft. I'll lay a place for myself near those rocks."

Glory nodded, understanding immediately. "Then what will we do in the morning?"

"You figure to keep the mine, work it?"

She glanced at the covered shape of her father. "Yes," she said in a decisive way. "Like you've said, it must be a valuable claim, and Pa spent all these years hoping to find one. Now that he's gone and it's left to me, it seems only right that I make the most of it, else all he went through was for nothing."

"Good. Was what I wanted you to say. We'll plan it all out tomorrow."

Glory looked again at the blanketed figures on the ground. "What about them?" she asked hesitantly.

"I'll take care of it. Can dig a couple of graves over there under that tree, bury them in the morning—unless you want to take your pa into Tombstone."

"No need, and I think he'd like it better out here where he made his strike."

Shawn moved up to Pete Lusky and, tucking the cover about the man's body, lifted it to his shoulder, and carried it to the spot he had chosen for the burial. Returning, he took up the slight shape of Ira Cannon, moved it to a place beside the old prospector.

When he came back the second time, Glory was bending over Cannon's chuck box, rummaging about in it for food.

"We'll have to eat," she said, half apologetically, as if to do so would be some sort of irreverent act.

"Sure. Can use what's in my saddlebags or Pete Lusky's grub sack if you don't find something in there. I'll fix you a fire behind the rocks."

Glory paused. The mound of boulders he had spoken of would hide her from the eyes of anyone down the slope.

"Do you think whoever that was might try again tonight?"

"Be hard to guess what somebody like that's thinking, but it wouldn't be a big surprise to me. Thing you've got to remember until I can run down whoever it is and take care of him, is that you're going to be in danger every minute. You can't take even the smallest chance of letting yourself be a target—"

"I can't live like that, Shawn!" Glory broke in. "I can't—won't crawl into a hole and hide!"

"Going to have to be about that bad," he replied in a patient voice. "Idea's to stay alive, enjoy what your pa left you, isn't it?"

"Of course—"

"Then you do what's best for you. Don't think it'll take long. That killer's bound to show his hand again and this time I'll be ready."

Shawn moved off, began to collect wood for a fire from the scraps of lumber discarded by Ira Cannon as he worked in the shaft, and which he had piled behind the rocks. There was no possibility of securing the area completely from a marksman who could, if he wished, get above them on the hillside, but by taking ordinary precautions, Glory would be fairly safe for the time being.

The fire going, Starbuck then corralled Lusky's burro with that of Cannon's, careful to avoid the cantankerous little beast's sharp teeth and flashing hooves, and then saw to the sorrel. That done, he made the necessary sleeping arrangements—the girl inside the mine, he in a shadowed area beyond the flare of firelight. By the time that was finished, Glory had a meal ready, and together they sat down to eat.

Lying just inside the mouth of the shaft, Glory Cannon stared upward through the opening at the starlit sky. The hush was near absolute, with not even the muted call of a night bird or the yap of a coyote breaking the blanket-like silence.

She wished she might have found some tears to shed over her father and knew that Shawn had wondered about the absence. But they simply wouldn't come; there had been only a sadness for his death, but it had gone no deeper.

She did remember the early days when he was around home, which was always an uncertain thing and never long established until they moved to Wickenburg. There'd been times then when they'd had fun together, but Ira Cannon was a man vagrant as the wind—here one day, gone the next. The nearest she'd ever come to really knowing him was during that time after her mother died when he had taken the job in the livery stable, a period embracing something less than a year; but that, too, ended when he drifted on after leaving her in the care of the Glasgows. His continuing absence thereafter had resulted in weaning him from her memory almost entirely.

Only the desire to get away from the Glasgows when she was past her mid-teens had prompted her to think of him again—and not because of any filial devotion but for the simple reason that he was the only remaining port in a sea of uncertainty that was closing in on her. She could, of course, have enlisted in the corps of soiled doves roosting in a house at the end of Front Street that was run by a woman known as Sadie May.

But she cared too little about men for that, a trait developed to a high degree, no doubt, by the wavering instability she had seen in her father and by certain experiences endured in her girlhood, and thus the only avenue open was to seek him out, compel him to afford her the home she had never actually had.

Such had occurred to her when word had come that Ira Cannon had been seen in Tombstone—a town, it was said, where everyone was fast becoming wealthy from the fabulous lodes of silver stored in the nearby hills. Ira Cannon could very well be numbered among those, and while in her own mind she had reservations as to that, she was desperate enough to gamble on anything; thus, she set out to find him . . . He was her father; he owed her a life, and she would have it.

But Glory hadn't anticipated meeting a man like Shawn Starbuck.

A warmth spread through her as she rolled to her stomach, raised her head, and looked toward the dark shape of him sleeping beyond the dead fire. Earlier, she had watched him as he stood, tall and inflexible at the rim of the flat, his face turned from her as he stared off into the night. She didn't need to see him to know exactly how he would look—dark, thick hair; eyes that were a pale gray some folks called a slate color; a full mustache overhanging a large mouth; a hard, square chin.

He was unbelievably strong and thoroughly capable, she had realized as she observed him working about the camp. He was able to do anything he set his hand to, yet he always wore a faintly distant expression, as if his thoughts were miles away and of such consequence that they removed him from all that was near.

There was something in his past, or perhaps it lay in the future, that apparently held him steadfast to some purpose. It could be the brother he mentioned, the one he was searching for, but she rather suspected it went beyond this—that it was a vast loneliness that beset him, placed him apart, and refused to let him participate in the ordinary ways of other men.

He was admittedly what she'd heard many people scornfully refer to as a drifter, but he was far removed from the sort said to possess no more in life than a "ten-dollar horse and a forty-dollar saddle." There was instead a solidness to him, an air of reassurance and confidence, and no man she had ever seen in her eighteen years of life intrigued and impressed her as did he.

She stirred, reliving those earlier minutes when they were walking down the crowded streets of Tombstone. Men looked at her there just as they had in Wickenburg and Tucson, with that hungry wanting in their eyes; but when they saw Starbuck, they turned away instantly, something in his manner warning them off.

It had given her a proud feeling, filled her with a singing elation; men instantly respected him, perhaps even feared him a little, and would think twice before forcing him to turn on them. Yet he was a gentle man. She recognized that not only in the way he treated her but in the patient care he accorded his horse and the two burros in the corral. Often, men were kind to women, even to other men, but where animals were concerned, they would be cruel and thoughtless. Shawn was different; he was like the giant in a fairy tale she remembered—strong and invincible, able to defy even the most powerful gods, yet kind and humble enough to pause and rescue a butterfly from a spider's silken trap.

She would not permit herself to think of his leaving, as he said he must. That thought she refused to admit, for without him, she could no longer envision a future, and whether the legacy of her father proved of value or not, life would be incomplete without him. With him, she felt secure, whole—and while he had not made the smallest overture, he also made her feel wanted, and that counted most of all.

Somehow, she would persuade him to stay. Finding his brother could not—should not—be more important than his own happiness.

TEN

Alone, Starbuck waited at the edge of the plateau for Glory. Early that morning, he had hollowed two graves out of the rocky hillside where the shade of several small trees laid a filigree pattern, and after wrapping the bodies of Ira Cannon and Pete Lusky in their blankets and bed tarps, he buried them. Later, he fashioned crosses, each with its appropriate name, and sank them deep in the dark soil.

Now, with all in order at the mine and ready for the short journey to Tombstone, he stood quietly by while Glory, seemingly on impulse, spent a few moments at her father's final resting place.

She was looking to him, Shawn knew, for advice and a plan as to what should next be done; he had as much as promised her he would think of something. But after a night's mulling it about, his mind was still barren, and he had no answer other than to return to the settlement and talk over her problems with John Trimm, their only acquaintance in Tombstone and the nearest thing to a close friend, apparently, that Ira Cannon had.

It was late morning when they turned into Allen Street and began to bull their way through the crowd toward the assayer's office. There appeared to be no letup in the constantly surging traffic, and the pall of gray dust floating over the town seemed thicker, if such was possible.

Several new buildings, half canvas, half board, had sprung into being in the short time they had been away, and one, a large square devoted to gambling, was already doing a brisk business with roulette, chuck-a-luck, monte, faro, and poker tables literally besieged by men anxious to pit their luck against the skills of the smooth, well-dressed gamblers.

At the corner of the street where Trimm's office stood, several Mexican laborers had begun to lay adobe blocks, starting what would be one of the first permanent-type structures, and on beyond it, a mule-drawn wagon loaded with clay bricks was discharging its cargo in preparation for another building of consequence.

Tombstone was already undergoing change, Starbuck realized. The thin board shacks, the tents, and the combination plank-and-canvas makeshifts were coming down almost as quickly as they went up, the time of replacement being only that period required to obtain material, hire labor, and construct a new edifice of substantial material.

"Will it ever stop?" Glory asked as they pulled up to the hitch rack fronting the assay office.

Starbuck, not hearing because of the rumbling passage of an ore wagon, looked at her questioningly as he dismounted.

"I was just wondering if the boom here would

ever end," she explained as he caught her under the arms and swung her lightly to the ground.

"It'll level off someday—all depending on how long the silver lasts," he replied, turning toward the building.

A dozen men—prospectors, engineers, several well-dressed individuals, and a few who looked to be no more than loafers—stood along the walk adjacent to Trimm's office. All paused to touch Starbuck and Glory Cannon with their glance as the pair stepped up onto the landing. A half a dozen more were inside the dusty room as they entered. Trimm, sitting at a table behind the counter, turned to face them, his eyes briefly showing surprise.

"You find Ira?" he asked, evidently quickly recalling Glory's identity.

The girl nodded. "He was dead—murdered. We found his body when we got there."

The room was in abrupt silence. Trimm rose, moved up to the counter, his attention reaching beyond them to the hitch rack. "You bring him in for burying?"

Starbuck shook his head. "No point in that. Miss Cannon thought it would be better to dig his grave there."

The assayer eyed them narrowly. One of the men standing next to the back wall turned, hurried out onto the walk, and began to speak in a low voice to those gathered there.

"Seems you were in something of a rush," Trimm observed dully. "Was only yesterday you were in here looking for Cannon. Now you're back, saying you found him, but he was dead. I'm beginning to wonder if—"

"Don't say it," Starbuck cut in coldly. "He was dead when we found him—and this lady *is* his daughter. She can prove it if she needs to. We're here for advice since you seem to have been a friend of Cannon's. If we've come to the wrong place, say so."

Trimm swallowed hard, shrugged. "What kind of advice?"

"What do we do next?"

Starbuck had purposely avoided mentioning the attempt on Glory's life that had resulted in the death of Pete Lusky. He could see no need, since there was no authority around to report either the attempt or the murder to—and as far as protection for the girl was concerned, that was up to him.

The assayer folded his arms, stepped back, and settled on the edge of his table. "You going to work the claim?"

Glory nodded. "It looked like Pa was about ready to begin. He'd got the shaft started and had put up some framing—"

"Shoring—"

"Whatever . . . Can you remember how much the ore Pa brought in for you to test was worth?"

"Four thousand dollars a ton—"

Shawn and Glory turned to the speaker, a fairly young blond man wearing corduroys, knee boots, and a narrow-brimmed peaked hat. There was a trace of accent in his voice—German, Starbuck thought.

"Excuse me," he continued, removing the headgear. "I have just heard of Ira Cannon's death and that you are his daughter. I am sorry."

"Did you know him?" Shawn asked, studying the man closely. Glory Cannon could expect a legion of acquaintances of her father to show up now, each claiming to be his trusted friend, perhaps even partner.

"Yes, he had hired me to supervise the working of his mine. I am Horst Kruger, an engineer. We were to begin today. I have already hired two laborers and we were waiting for him—your father—to come for us."

Starbuck listened skeptically. After a bit, he stirred. "That's a good story and like as not it's true. But we'll need a little proof."

Kruger reached into the pocket of his coat, drew forth a folded sheet of paper, and handed it to Shawn.

"I understand," he said. "Here is a list of supplies Ira ordered me to get from Murchison's store and have ready. It is signed by him."

Starbuck glanced at the smudged paper and passed it to the girl. She smiled wryly.

"I don't know Pa's signature. He never once wrote."

Horst Kruger rubbed at his clean-shaven jaw. "Well, there is Murchison himself. He will vouch for me . . . And there are others—"

"This Murchison will do fine," Shawn said, wheeling to face the crowd in the office. "Where do we find him?"

Glory caught at his arm. "I think we ought to let him go ahead, start the work or whatever it is that he does. Pa must have trusted him."

"Way I see it, too. You'll have to have somebody running things for you—but I'm all for making sure. There's no doubt now your pa's claim is a good one and—"

"What's this about, Ira Cannon?" a strong voice boomed from the doorway. "I want to talk to whoever brought in that story!"

Starbuck smiled down at the girl. "The buzzards are showing up fast," he murmured. "This one'll probably claim he's half-owner."

ELEVEN

He was a big man, and his strident voice matched his bulk. Around middle age, he had small, dark eyes, thin lips, a spade beard, and neatly trimmed mustache. The expensive-looking brown suit he wore was covered with a film of Tombstone's lime dust.

"You the woman claiming to be Cannon's daughter?" he demanded, pulling up in front of Glory.

The girl bristled. "I am his daughter," she snapped. "Who the hell are you?"

Starbuck grinned. This was the Glory Cannon who had surprised him in his camp with an unloaded shotgun.

A titter ran through the office, and the big man recoiled, somewhat taken aback. He brushed at his mustache.

"I'm T. J. Yorkan. Lawyer. Handled the legal work for Ira Cannon. Can you prove you're his daughter?"

"She can," Starbuck said. "Can you prove what you're saying?"

"Yes, sir. Can show you copies of his papers. You the husband?"

"A friend. What kind of legal work did you do for Ira Cannon?"

"Helped him with his filing and with getting set up at the mill and the bank at Bisbee . . . Indians get Ira?"

"Could've been," Shawn said, throwing a warning glance at Glory.

It was wise, he thought, to reveal little of what they knew; the man who had slain Ira Cannon and tried to cut down Glory could be among those in that very room. Later, if T. J. Yorkan proved to be trustworthy, he would make a full accounting of the prospector's death so far as he and the girl could supply, and also include the details on that of Pete Lusky. Such information should be filed with the law once an office was established.

"Too bad," Yorkan said. "Ira was all set to hit it big. Prospects were good, too." The lawyer paused, glanced about. Trimm and the dozen or so onlookers were listening interestedly to all that was being said. "Let's get outside. Find a little more privacy there than in here."

Stepping back, he made a gesture toward the door. Glory moved by him, and the attorney, ignoring Starbuck and Horst Kruger, fell in behind her. Shawn, with the engineer at his heels, nodded to Trimm and followed the pair out onto the walk.

"Got no office yet," Yorkan stated loudly. "Can't find a carpenter to start building one for me. Saloon and gambling house people are all offering so blamed much money for a day's work that ordinary folks can't hire anybody. We're outbid, you might say. Have to conduct my business on the street . . . Like to know what you have in mind, little lady."

Starbuck shook his head. "Don't see as that concerns you."

"Expect it does. Be some paperwork to be done. Inheritance, passing title to the property on to the heir, things like that. Important that everything be kept absolutely straight. Been quite a few claims jumped, all legal, simply because they'd been improperly handled at the start."

Shawn glanced at Kruger. "That right?"

The engineer, his eyes at the moment on Glory, nodded hastily. "It is so. It is wise to be careful."

"Wondering, too," Yorkan continued, "if you plan to work the claim or if you want to sell out. I'm in touch with several Eastern capitalists, all with plenty of money to invest in a good mine."

Glory said, "No, not what I had in mind."

"Then maybe you'll be looking for a partner—"

"Shawn—Mr. Starbuck, here, is my partner. I don't want another—and Mr. Kruger is going to run things for us, get the ore out."

"I see," the lawyer said briskly. "You're all set."

Starbuck was considering the girl in silence. He hadn't missed her words; *partner* she had called him—and nothing was further from his own wishes. He hoped she had made the statement only as a means to forestall further insistence on the part of Yorkan.

"But I will want you to fix up whatever papers are necessary to show that the mine belongs to me—"

"Of course, of course. Be glad to. Now as to cash money, you have enough to get things underway, I assume."

The girl glanced at Starbuck, an expression of dejection crossing her features. "No, I have only a dollar or two." She turned to Kruger. "Will it take much?"

The engineer frowned, "Will take some, Miss Cannon—"

"Glory—"

"Glory," Kruger repeated, flushing slightly. "We will have to feed the men, but that won't take much. And there are tools that will be needed, and lumber."

"Where was Pa getting money for all that? I've never known him to have any cash—at least not more than a dollar or two."

"We hadn't got that far," Kruger said. "He hoped to persuade Murchison to give credit, back him long enough to get out a few tons of ore."

"Murchison wouldn't have done it," Yorkan said flatly. "Know him. Been several go to him with the same proposition. Turned them all down. He's in the general merchandise business, not banking."

"I can get by, wait for my wages," Kruger said. "And the Mexican fellows won't expect to be paid for a week. But we'll need the lumber and tools—and food."

"All at a premium around here," Yorkan said. "You know that, Kruger. Suppliers are getting ten times the regular price for everything they sell—and they demand spot cash. If a man can't come up with it, they forget him. Always somebody waiting to buy that has the money."

Shawn faced the girl. "Can talk to this Murchison anyway, if you want. Could be your pa made some arrangements with him."

"Afraid he didn't," Kruger said before Glory could make an answer. "Was to be part of my job, convince the store owner that the mine was a good one and he'd not be running any risk."

"He would've still turned you down," the lawyer said decisively. "Makes it a policy to stay out of the mining end of it. Figures to make his pile supplying the suckers and the lucky ones who've hit it . . . Could be I can give you some help—"

A rattle of gunshots at the Allen Street corner cut into the attorney's words. A few of the men on the walk nearby began to move toward the sound, but most merely glanced in that direction, conversations scarcely interrupted.

"How?" Starbuck asked suspiciously.

Yorkan hesitated, studied Shawn narrowly. "You have something to say in this, or does the mine belong to Miss Cannon?"

Starbuck's eyes flickered. He didn't care much for the lawyer and was not sure that he could be trusted.

"Let's put it this way," he said, "I'm looking out for her. Keep that in mind."

"I see," Yorkan said crisply. "Always like to have a clear understanding."

"What about helping me—us?" Glory asked. "How can you?"

"Well, happens I'm not like George Murchison. I'm not averse to doing a bit of investing on the side as long as I know what I'm getting into—and I get paid for the use of my money. I know Ira Cannon's claim is a good one, could even be one of the richer mines."

"That mean you'd be willing to make a loan on it?"

"Let's say I'm willing to talk about it. Warning you now, however, I don't do such things out of the goodness of my heart."

"Which means your interest rate will be high," Starbuck observed dryly.

"It'll fall right in line with everything else here in Tombstone—supplies, lumber, whiskey, labor—you name it. If it's something you have to buy, you'll pay dear for it. Why, that sorrel horse standing there, I expect the owner could get a thousand dollars for it from somebody that was needing him!"

Starbuck wagged his head. He'd paid five double-eagles for the gelding and figured that was high.

"Mules are even more valuable," Kruger said. "Heard of a fellow paying twenty-five hundred for a team and wagon a few days ago."

"Was fortunate to even find a man who'd sell them to him," Yorkan said, and nodded to Glory. "You interested in doing business with me?"

The girl turned to Starbuck. "What do you think? I can't see that there's any other way we can get started."

"Expect it's the only answer," Shawn agreed. "Cash is what you need, and the only way to get it is borrow. If the mine's as good as they say, it wouldn't take you long to pay off . . . That the way you see it?" he added, shifting his attention to Horst Kruger.

The engineer nodded. "It is a good mine, I think."

"Then you think I should go ahead?" Glory asked, still speaking to Starbuck.

"Only way you'll be able to work your claim, and I don't reckon Yorkan's price will be any higher than any other man's."

Yorkan slapped his hands together. "Fine! One of the stores is letting me use a storage room when I need to sit down and make out papers. Can go there now and get started."

Glory reached for Starbuck's wrist as he stepped back. "You're coming with me, aren't you?"

"No point," Shawn replied.

He had already become much too deeply involved in Glory Cannon's problems for his own good. Now that it appeared that she, with the assistance of Horst Kruger and lawyer Yorkan, would be able to manage, it was time he turned his attention to his own affairs. Not that he intended to forsake the girl entirely; it was still too soon for that, but she should be made to realize that he would be around for but a short while.

"But I'll need you to—"

"Kruger knows all about the mine, can furnish any information that's necessary—and me being along won't change the kind of deal Yorkan will give you."

"But where are you going—what are you planning to do?"

"Aim to ask around about my brother. Was what I came here for in the first place. Probably be gone a couple of hours."

"We'll be finished long before that," the lawyer said. "Once the paperwork's done, you'll probably want to go to Murchison's and arrange for your supplies. Might suggest you all meet there."

"That's a good idea," Kruger agreed.

Disconsolate, Glory turned away. "All right," she murmured. "We'll wait there for you."

Starbuck smiled, nodded, turned to the engineer. "Take care of her," he said, and wheeling, started back up the walk for Allen Street.

TWELVE

Reaching the intersection, Shawn turned into the traffic- and dust-choked thoroughfare and angled for a large board and canvas structure immediately to his right. It was jammed with patrons, and as he entered the dirt-floored building the sound of music being hammered out on a piano buried somewhere in the confusion reached him. Along with the faintly audible rhythm, he heard also the solid stomp of booted feet keeping time.

Shouldering his way deeper into the carnival-like surroundings, he located the dance floor, a square wooden platform built at ground level in the center of the area. Its surface was crowded with couples, all swaying and rocking back and forth energetically to the strains of the tune being played. The bar, a long raw-lumber counter with unfinished shelves behind it, stood beyond, and Starbuck, again putting his shoulder foremost, drove a course for it.

A half-dozen bartenders were pouring drinks. Sweat glistened on their haggard features, and they all moved about as if in a daze, their senses dulled by the constant clamor and commotion, the hovering mixture of smoke and dust. A seventh man, wearing a soiled white shirt and a black string tie, a pistol tucked under the waistband of his pants, was at the end of the bar accepting money handed to him by the countermen and dropping it into a metal cash box.

Finally getting his shot glass of watered whiskey, Shawn moved to where the cashier, undoubtedly the saloon's proprietor, had established his position. He nodded to the man and smiled.

"Like to buy you a drink."

The saloon man studied him coldly. "Never touch the stuff," he said, shrugging. "I'm Jake Aldridge. You looking for me?"

Shawn took a swallow of the whiskey. "Could be you're smart. I've made coffee stronger'n this."

Humor was no part of Jake Aldridge. "They don't know the difference," he said, jerking his head at the crowd. "Who are you and what do you want? If it's a job—"

"Name's Starbuck and I'm not looking for work. Trying to locate my brother. Calls himself Damon Friend, or maybe Ben Starbuck. Expected to find him here in Tombstone."

"Never heard of him. What's he do?"

"Most anything, probably. Has put on a boxing match now and then, but I don't think he makes a living at it."

Aldridge glanced up to one of the several improvised chandeliers hanging from beams stretching like a cross from the canvas ceiling. Three of the oil lamps affixed to it had gone out, and a fourth was now smoking from lack of fuel.

All the while, he was minding the steady flow of coins coming to him from the bartender. The foot-square cash box was half full of money.

"Still don't mean anything to me," he said. "You tried anywhere else?"

"This is the first place in town I've asked. Been looking for him for years."

"Must be mighty important—"

"Matter of settling the family estate. Can't be done until I get him back home to sign some papers."

Aldridge looked up again at the thirsting lamp. It had stopped smoking. "Well, if I hear of somebody by them names, I'll mention you. Where'll you be?"

"The Glory Mine, about five miles up the valley."

"You working a claim?"

"No, just helping out a lady for a few days, then I'll be riding on. Obliged to you."

The saloon man nodded, and Starbuck wheeled, beat his way back through the crush to the street.

At the next four saloons, all varying little except that two offered gambling, he met with no better success than in Aldridge's. But in the fifth, a bartender, noting the buckle he was wearing—a silver oblong upon which was mounted an ivory likeness of a boxer posed in classic stance—expressed an interest.

"Sure is a fine bit of jewelry you got there . . .

You one of them fancy-dan kind of fighters?"

"Know a little about it," Shawn answered. "Was my pa that was the expert. He gave me and my brother a few lessons."

"He the one you're hunting?"

"Yeah. Been known to put on boxing exhibitions—maybe has right here. You ever hear of him?"

"Nope, can't say as I have, but there's a big jasper that hangs around Melly Jones's place who claims he's a champion of something or somewhere. Seen him go a few rounds here a couple of weeks ago. Pretty good, I reckon, if you like that kind of fighting. Me, I figure a man ought to go at it the best way he can and—"

"What's his name?" Starbuck cut in, coming to attention.

"Charley something-or-other . . . Fisk, maybe it was."

Likely it wasn't Ben. The bartender would have noticed a resemblance that Shawn had been told was strong between himself and his brother. But if Charley followed the boxing trail, he very well could know of Ben and possibly where he might be found.

"Melly Jones's place—where is it?"

"End of Tough Nut Street. Just keep heading straight when you go out the door till there ain't nothing, then turn left. You'll spot it standing off sort of by itself."

Starbuck moved out at once. He hadn't even begun to visit all of the saloons and gambling halls roaring away at full tilt in the settlement, probably would need a couple more days to do so, but he'd made a start.

There was less of a crowd tramping Tombstone's outer area, and while Melly Jones, a dark, oily-faced man with a large girth, was not enjoying the staggering load of business Starbuck had witnessed in the establishments on Allen Street, his place, nevertheless, had an ample share.

Finding the saloon man at a corner table engaged in a hand of poker, Shawn introduced himself and asked for Charley. Jones jerked a thumb at a thick-set, bull-necked man slouching against the counter. Face turned away, he was talking to several men who were laughing as he related some incident that apparently involved him. Elsewhere in the building other card games were in progress, but there was no music, no dance floor, and no women.

Starbuck ordered himself a drink from one of the two bartenders and took a position near Charley. Waiting until there was a lull in the conversation, he caught the man's eye and nodded.

"Hear you've spent some time in the ring."

The boxer, a solid, battered-faced individual with jet-black hair and close-cropped beard, came fully around and hooked his elbows on the edge of the counter. With calm deliberation, he assessed Shawn from head to toe.

"Do for a fact," he said. "That buckle you're wearing mean you're in the fight game?"

"No," Starbuck replied, and made his explanation as to how he had come by it. "Have a brother that could be, however. Wanted to ask if you knew him. Name's Ben Starbuck, but he calls himself Damon Friend, too."

Charley's rugged features drew into a scowl. "Been a lot of places, done a lot of fighting, but I don't recollect nobody by them names."

"I'm told we look quite a bit alike—"

Charley again swept Starbuck with his glance. "Nope, ain't never seen nobody looking like you, either. You a boxer, too?"

"Only when I have to be."

"Was thinking we might put on a little show. Way things are around here, expect we'd clean up pretty good. Galoots in this burg've got money burning holes in their pockets."

Shawn grinned, "Appreciate the offer, but I'll have to pass."

"Why? You got a job or something you can't get away from?"

A squat, slovenly man in overalls standing next to the boxer laughed. "Hell, he ain't no damn fool, Charley! Knows he'd not stand a chance against the likes of you. That there belt buckle's just for show."

"Said it belonged to his pa, didn't he?"

"Yep, and he said his pa had learned him how to fight, too—"

Starbuck swallowed the last of his drink, set the glass on the counter. The man in the overalls was slightly drunk, and the liquor was filling him with false bravery.

"Hell, I'm betting I could take him," he declared abruptly and lunged forward.

Shawn threw up an arm. Palm open, fingers spread, he caught the man in the face, shoved hard. The drunk went staggering backward, tripped over his own feet, and sat down solidly on the dirt floor. A roar of laughter went up from the men at the bar and others close by, and from across the room the voice of Melly Jones sounded.

"Goddammit, Parker—if you're starting another one of your ruckuses, get out! I'm tired of fixing tables and buying chairs, you hear?"

Parker, his face a flaming red, was struggling to his feet. A man down the counter yelled, "Ain't nothing to worry about, Melly! Whatever he was starting got finished mighty quick!"

"Picked on the wrong tomcat this time, he did," someone added.

"The hell—" Parker shouted and rushed for Starbuck, both fists swinging. Shawn stepped aside, easily avoiding the blows. He flung a glance at Charley. The boxer's crushed features were expressionless.

Parker, mouthing curses, spun and came in again as the patrons in the saloon began to form a ring about the two men. Shawn nailed the man with a quick left, stalled him, followed with half a dozen more jabbing lefts, and then a solid right to the belly.

Parker reeled back against the bar, mouth flared open as he gasped for breath, thick arms hanging loosely at his sides. Melly Jones was again shouting, but his words were lost in the cheering and babble of talk.

Starbuck stood quiet for a long minute, eyes on Parker. The man had had enough, he saw, and then he swung his attention to Charley.

"You ever run across my brother, I'll appreciate your telling him I'm looking for him."

"Sure will," the boxer said, admiration showing in his eyes. "Was as pretty a hammering as I've ever seen. Any chance of you changing your mind and us putting on a show for the town? Be willing to split fifty-fifty."

"Job I've got's going to keep me busy for a spell," Shawn replied and, pushing through the circle of onlookers, left the saloon.

He would have to resume asking about Ben another time, he realized, glancing at the sun. Glory and Horst Kruger would by that hour have completed their business with Yorkan and be waiting for him.

Moving on to Allen, he joined the throng once

again and fought his way to the side street on which John Trimm's office stood. He saw the girl waiting on the landing when he rounded the corner. She was looking anxiously in his direction for him. He sighed heavily. Glory Cannon was going to be a problem.

THIRTEEN

Glory spotted him when he was still a dozen yards away and ran to meet him. Her eyes were bright with relief, and she was brimming with happiness.

"Oh, Shawn—everything is all fixed!" she cried. "I've borrowed enough from Mr. Yorkan to get all we need, even rent a team of mules and a wagon to haul the ore! The lumber is already on the way."

Starbuck grinned, held up both hands. "Slow down! You're going too fast for me."

She laughed, seized him by an arm. "It's going to work out fine for us—all of us."

"Can be sure of it, and you'll like as not end up a rich woman. What kind of a deal did you get from Yorkan?"

"Loaned me ten thousand dollars—*ten thousand!* I never knew there was that much money! It'll be enough to handle everything."

"How much interest is he charging you?"

"Twenty-five percent," Glory replied as they halted before the smiling Kruger. "I have to repay the loan in fifteen days."

Shawn frowned, whistled softly. "That the best you could do?" he asked, shifting his attention to the engineer.

Kruger nodded. "From what I have heard, it is the usual rate charged. We made objections, but he would not listen."

"Not what I'm thinking about—it's that two-week deadline. What happens if you don't meet it?"

"The mine is forfeited. That is the collateral he insisted on."

"Pretty stiff—"

"It was accept his terms or nothing," Kruger said. "And Glory thought that if we could not make the mine pay off in fifteen days, we'd know it was worthless, and Yorkan could have it."

"He's pretty sure the claim's a good one," Shawn said thoughtfully, "otherwise he would've never laid out that much money, interest or not. I don't figure T. J. Yorkan as a man with a big heart."

"Then you think I did things right?" Glory asked hesitantly.

"You did fine, but we've got to get busy, get that ore out and down to the mill. Two weeks won't give us much time."

"Horst says it won't be too hard to meet the note if everything goes the way it should."

"Just what we've got to sidestep—things going wrong . . . You say the lumber you need is already on the way to the mine?"

Kruger nodded. "We stopped a load coming in from the mountains. The driver was a man

I knew, and I persuaded him to sell it to us."

"And we've got the supplies all bought up. They're being loaded in the wagon now."

"What about the two laborers?"

"They rode out with the lumber."

Starbuck smiled again. "You two are way ahead of me. Sounds like we're all ready to start mining."

"We are," Glory agreed, and then added, "What about your brother? Did you find any trace of him?"

"None. Asked at about a half-dozen places, had no luck. Just have to keep trying."

"Glory has told me of him," Kruger said. "To find him in this town where there are so many men, it will be a hard job . . . I think it is best we get started for the mine. It isn't good to be on the road with supplies after dark."

"You go ahead," Glory said quickly. "I'll ride with Shawn. Some things I want to talk to him about."

Kruger gave her a courteous bow and turned away at once. Starbuck watched him disappear into the swirl of traffic, then looked back at the girl.

"Talk to me about what?"

"The mine—our working together. I want you to take charge of getting the ore to the mill. I can drive the wagon; you will be the guard. Horst says we'll need one. Outlaws are always hiding out along the way, hoping to steal a load of rich ore."

"Be one reason to let the regular haulers carry it for you. Don't think anybody would ever try hijacking one of those big rigs."

"That's what we'll do as soon as we get enough production. They won't bother with just a couple of tons, and that's all we'll have at the start . . . I asked Horst what a job like that paid—being a guard, I mean. He said a hundred dollars a trip would be about right."

"Seems like plenty—"

"But it'll be worth every cent of it to me. Later, after we get to where we're shipping a lot of ore and the big haulers are handling it, I'd still want you to oversee it all—not let them cheat us or anything like that."

Starbuck took the girl by the hand, moved toward the hitch rack where the sorrel waited in slack-hipped patience.

"I appreciate your figuring me in on all this, Glory, but you've got to understand that I won't be around for long—just until I find Ben or know for sure that he's not here."

Her step dragged. "But that will take only a few days! Wouldn't it be smart to stay for a longer time—a month even? He might show up."

"Got my doubts. If he's not on a job somewhere, he would have been here by now. If he is, it's not likely he'd quit."

Glory's voice was low, pleading. "Shawn, please stay for a while—at least two weeks."

Starbuck raised his eyes, stared out across the dust-blurred hills. He had promised himself earlier to look after the girl, protect her, and track down the killer who had made an attempt on her life; the need was probably even more critical now—and he could not leave with that threat hanging over her. Besides, it would take several days, in his spare time, to visit all of the town's remaining saloons and gambling halls in his search for Ben.

"Yeah, reckon I could manage that, all right—"

Impulsively, Glory turned and threw her arms about his neck. Drawing him down, she kissed him. Nearby, several men laughed and clapped. Starbuck grinned, nodded to them and, freeing the leathers from the hitch rack's bar, got into the saddle. Then, reaching down for the girl, he swung her up behind him.

"Some jaspers have all the luck," a voice from the sidewalk commented.

Shawn smiled again and, bucking his head at John Trimm, who was standing in the window of his office watching, pulled the gelding about.

"Bought myself some new clothes, too," Glory said happily as they swung off toward the main street. "Felt I just couldn't wear these old rags any longer. They're in the wagon with the rest of the supplies."

Starbuck barely heard as they threaded a course along the noisy, bustling street. "You have any trouble while I was gone?" he asked. "There anybody you noticed that seemed to be paying a lot of attention to you?"

"A couple of men tried to shine up to me while we were waiting. Horst got kind of mad at them—like he was jealous."

"Maybe he was," Shawn said. "What I'm talking about is if you saw anybody following you, sort of keeping tabs on you."

His tone sobered her. "You're thinking about that killer—"

"I am—and we're not forgetting him for a minute. Somebody wants your mine, and he's willing to kill to get it."

She was silent for a long time. Then, "I didn't see anybody, Shawn. I guess I wasn't really looking—I was so happy about getting everything all fixed up. I promise I'll be more careful—"

"Just what we're both going to do, starting right now," Starbuck said, pulling the sorrel to a halt. Throwing a leg over, he dropped to the ground.

"Want you in the saddle. I'll ride behind. That way, I'll be covering you from anybody that might slip up behind us. Can also see who's ahead."

Glory worked herself over the cantle of the hull and settled in the deep seat. Starbuck vaulted up into place behind her.

"I'm going to like this," she murmured as his arms, reaching forth to grasp the reins, went around her.

Horst Kruger, on the seat of the converted farm wagon, lines slack in his hands as the mules jogged steadily along the road leading to the Glory Mine, thought back over the past hours.

When the news reached him that Ira Cannon was dead, his hopes had plunged. Another opportunity lost, another failure even before he had the chance to fail. It was to be a final attempt to do something with his life, and he had already made up his mind that should it not work out, he was finished once and for all with the effort.

He was a good mining engineer; he was certain of that, yet nothing had ever gone right for him. On his three previous jobs, circumstances had done nothing to help his professional standing. A series of accidents on one; some miscalculations, not all his fault, but for which he bore the blame, on another; and a skillfully salted gold mine that he had been led to certify as bona fide forced him to keep a low profile.

Shortly after his last job, he had drifted into Tombstone, arriving not long after Ed Schieffelin, a black-bearded *landsman,* had made his strikes. But reputation tagged him relentlessly, and he had no luck in getting in with any of the big mining syndicates and partnerships that were blossoming hourly in the booming settlement. It took him but very little time to learn that talent can be obscured by errors, however honest, and awaken to the fact that he was being shunned by men who needed his service desperately.

And then he met Ira Cannon. A meek little man, equally a loser and failure, he was finding it hard to believe that, at last, he had scored and was on the verge of riches. Horst had applied to him for work when he overheard Cannon, somewhat in his cups, outlining plans to work his claim. Ira had hired him without question.

Kruger had seen no reason to enumerate the black marks of the past, feeling certain that there were those in Tombstone who had already called such to Cannon's attention. If so, it mattered nothing to Ira, for he never mentioned it, simply instructed his engineer to proceed with plans at all possible haste. In Horst Kruger, he perhaps recognized a man such as himself, forever down and out and in need of a break, and had extended a compassionate hand.

But misfortune is an implacable enemy; Ira Cannon was murdered. The report stunned Kruger, figuratively drove him to his knees, but he rose quickly—and this time with a new determination rushing through him.

If only hard luck and disappointment were to be his reward in a life of diligence and honesty, then, by the gods, he should cross over to the other side! He was weary of poverty, of being stranded on the outer fringes of wealth; he was fed up with hard work, with mistakes, with blame, with just being another engineer—and one of no stature at that.

Horst Kruger had been in that frame of mind when the proposal was made to him—a scheme by which, as a partner, he would end up with one half of all the riches he could extract from Ira Cannon's mine. *One half!* The very thought staggered him. It could mean a million dollars, possibly more.

To claim it, he had only to profess friendship for Cannon's heir, a mere slip of a girl who didn't know a stope from a bucket of feldspar, and who had put in a totally unexpected appearance, and induce her to let him continue in the capacity he had been hired.

Thus, supervising the operation, his partner had pointed out, it would be simple to fool the girl, and in a short time, they would be in a position to take possession of the mine.

The plan had progressed without a hitch. Glory Cannon had honored the agreement he'd made with her father, and he was assuming command. Starbuck, the big hard-case she had brought with her, had not been so readily favorable, but he had deferred to her, and while he could be a source of later trouble, he, also, knew little if anything about mining for silver, and so it should not be hard to fool him as well.

Horst stirred restlessly on the hard seat of the wagon. That was all to the good. They were trusting him, and in so doing they had set him on the road to riches—but could he adhere to that course? Why was it that everywhere he looked, he seemed to see Glory Cannon smiling at him?

FOURTEEN

Work at the mine got underway that next morning. The first thing on the agenda, at Starbuck's insistence, was the erection of a high fence-like border around three sides of the plateau fronting the shaft. Made of brush and lumber, it would be ineffectual in stopping a bullet, but it would serve to shield Glory from the eyes of a would-be sniper hiding on the opposite slopes.

There was little that could be done to neutralize the rock ridge farther up on the hillside, however, and Shawn could only caution the girl as well as Kruger and the laborers to be on the alert at all times for any movement in the area.

Mounting the barricade and throwing up a small lean-to for the girl took all of that first day, but with the dawn of the second day, actual mining began. Only a simple, temporary arrangement for bringing out the ore and loading it into the wagon would be set up now, Kruger—who appeared to have a broad knowledge of the business—explained. Such would enable them to get a few tons to the stamp mill in a short time.

Once that was done and the Damoclean sword of the mortgage suspended over their heads by T. J. Yorkan was paid off, they would then get properly organized. Kruger had plans involving such things as A-frames, burro-powered traveling buckets, hoppers, and the like, which he intended to build once the pressure was off. They would speed up the mining process and make it much easier for all concerned.

For the time being, no structures other than the crude shelter for the girl would be put up. The men laid bedrolls on the ground in the open, and cooking was done over a rock-encircled pit across which a grating had been placed. Such arrangements, too, were for short duration, and would be improved upon as soon as those all-important first tons of ore were delivered to the Charleston stamp mill, the silver rendered, and T. J. Yorkan paid off and out of the picture.

On the afternoon of the third day, with Horst Kruger and the laborers working feverishly to build up a stockpile, Starbuck saddled the sorrel and made ready to ride out. Finishing with the chore, he turned to find Glory watching him intently, question in her eyes.

"Taking a ride down to that mill," he explained. "Like to see what the country's like between here and there."

Relief flooded her features at once, and he realized that she was afraid he had decided to leave.

"Be gone a couple of hours or so," he added.

The girl smiled. "Supper'll be at dark."

"I'll be here," he said, and mounting, rode

down the trail past the wagon and the corral they had thrown up for the mules, and out into the valley.

He swung southward, veering toward the San Pedro River. The road being taken now by ore haulers led through Tombstone itself, as most of the mines were close by or in the settlement itself. Cannon's claim was a distance from the town, however, and such would make it possible to avoid it and the consequent notice that would be taken of their passage.

Although he had said little about it, the conviction had grown in Starbuck's mind that efforts, in addition to the possibility of hijacking by outlaws, would be made to halt the delivery of those first tons of ore to the stamp mill. To him, it was only logical; someone had murdered Ira Cannon, and when it became known that Glory was his heir and successor—word that undoubtedly had spread quickly—an attempt was made on her life. The meaning of such was only too apparent; someone desperately wanted the mine.

Therefore, it followed naturally that failing to remove the girl from the scene, and finding her well protected, whoever it was would now take steps to prevent her from making a success of the venture by the simple process of intercepting the shipments, forcing her into bankruptcy, and making the claim available.

Just who the person or persons behind it all

might be was not an easily solved puzzle. With numberless men in the area, many of whom would be bent on gaining wealth by any means available, suspects were unlimited. Any man without a claim of his own or with one that had proven worthless could be a prospect.

And among them should be included T. J. Yorkan. He was one whose name came near the top of the list, if such should be made, Shawn felt. The lawyer had not hesitated to offer his backing to Glory when he became aware that she was in need of cash. He had readily advanced a large sum to her, which proved that he knew the Cannon mine was valuable. And he had secured his investment by binding the girl to an agreement that would make the property his if any problems developed in the brief time he was allotting for repayment.

He might be no more than a sharp businessman, out to make high interest on a short-term loan, one he secured by collateral he considered to be sufficient—but on the other hand, there could be more to it.

No one but Ira Cannon and he could say what was between them before the miner fell victim to a rifle bullet. Did Yorkan know certain things about the mine—that it possibly was as rich as those discovered by Schieffelin and others like him, for instance, and had he set out to get the property for himself? No one but he could answer that since Cannon was now dead, and certainly the lawyer would say nothing.

And if it were true, he undoubtedly could be considered more than just a suspect in the death of Cannon and likely had laid plans to take over the prospector's claim, which had been upset when Glory put in her appearance. It became necessary then to remove her; that had failed, and as a final alternative, he had provided the girl with a financing program so restrictive in its time limitation that a few manufactured delays would make him sole owner of the property.

It was all conjecture, of course. Starbuck admitted that as he rode slowly down the valley, but he was overlooking nothing. Yorkan could be, as he'd told himself, no more than a good businessman—but he would bear watching, nevertheless. Glory had only to fail in getting that small but necessary amount of ore to the mill to lose everything.

Taking a different route to Charleston would not be difficult, he saw. Faint wagon tracks were visible following along the cottonwood-edged river, and there were no excessively steep grades to be overcome by the mules. The hills, while rough with rock, long-stalked ocotillo, rambling beds of prickly pear and gaunt cholla cactus, mesquite and greasewood clumps, would pose no problem.

He rode on, mentally outlining a trail until he

reached the settlement on the banks of the river, and then turned back, retracing his own path. Soon, he was again near the side draw in which Ira Cannon had made his strike.

It had occurred to Starbuck to detour by Tombstone, make more inquiries relative to Ben, but time had slipped by, and now it was too late. Perhaps, after the meal was finished, he would do so.

The grinding sound of iron-tired wheels slicing into the soil and the thud of hooves reached Shawn as he swung toward the canyon in which the mine lay. Immediately, he pulled off into the brush and halted. Shortly, a buggy drawn by a single horse and occupied by two men came into view. Starbuck's attention sharpened. One of the passengers was T. J. Yorkan. Moving back into the open, he waited for the vehicle to draw abreast.

"Good to see you again," the lawyer said, pulling to a stop.

Shawn nodded. The lawyer had been to the mine. Undoubtedly, he had made a call for the purpose of seeing how much progress had been made.

"Like to have you meet a friend of mine—from New York . . . Aaron Bailey."

Bailey, a lean, prosperous-looking man with cottony muttonchops, leaned toward to better see out from beneath the buggy's top and smiled.

"My pleasure—"

Shawn acknowledged the introduction, his thoughts elsewhere. Yorkan had not waited long to look in on his investment. Was he worried about it—or had he come to find out when the first load of ore would be dispatched to the stamp mill?

"Mr. Bailey's interested in investing in the silver-mining business," Yorkan said. "I've been showing him around the country . . . Things seem to be coming along first rate at the Cannon place."

"We'll make it," Shawn replied.

The lawyer bobbed his head and settled back on the seat. "Well, good luck," he said and slapped the horse with the reins. "That's all it takes, along with plenty of hard work."

The New York man raised his hand in salute, smiled faintly as the buggy moved on. Starbuck remained motionless for a time, watching the vehicle until it disappeared into the distance, and then roweling the sorrel, resumed the trail to the mine. He was still pondering Yorkan's intentions when he turned into the clearing.

FIFTEEN

On the morning of the fifth day, the wagon was loaded, and they were ready for the initial haul to Charleston.

Glory, efficiently dressed in her new corduroy riding skirt, plaid shirt, boots, and light wool jacket, a flat-crowned hat on her head, took her place on the seat and gathered up the reins. Starbuck, armed not only with his pistol but also carrying a rifle, settled beside her.

He would have much preferred to have Kruger or one of the Mexican laborers driving the team, but the need to get out the ore, which was not going as well as hoped, and to be ready for the second trip to the mill, was paramount; thus, there was no choice but to let the girl handle the mules.

He saw quickly that he need have no fears insofar as her ability to drive the wagon was concerned. She maneuvered the vehicle out of the wash and down onto the more level floor of the valley with little difficulty and soon had the team and wagon moving at a steady pace along the river.

Shawn, the rifle riding across his knees, kept a careful watch on all sides for possible trouble, but they encountered no one. Most of the mining activity was taking place on the opposite side of the valley, and while now and then they did see men working the dark slopes and hear ore wagons rumbling toward Tombstone, they found themselves alone.

"You're worried about someone trying to stop us, take the ore," Glory observed not long after they were underway. "Did you run into something along here the other day that makes you think we might be held up?"

Starbuck shook his head. "No, just got a suspicious nature, I reckon . . . Not sure you realize how important it is that we get through."

"I know I'll lose the mine if we don't," she replied soberly.

"Just what it amounts to—and there's still that sniper. Not knowing who he is for sure makes it bad."

Glory looked at Starbuck quickly and frowned. "It sounds like you've got an idea who it is."

"No, just keep trying to think who it might be."

She was quiet for a long moment, then, "Sometimes I get the feeling that I can't win—that I'm meant to be a loser, like Pa."

"Wrong way to look at it. That killer's maybe given up—and we're going to get this load through. All we have to do is keep our eyes peeled. If anything does start—shooting, I mean—you get down under the seat, leave the team to me."

Glory's chin firmed. "You'll be busy with your gun. Driving the mules is my job."

A silence fell between them after that, and for the next few miles nothing was said. Finally, she turned to Starbuck.

"Have you thought any more about staying—about taking my offer to be a partner? I know you said you had to find your brother, but is it so important?

"Is to me," Shawn answered, and explained why it was necessary.

When he had finished, Glory shrugged and pushed her hat to the back of her head. "That could wait, couldn't it? You've gone this long without finding him. Would another year make a difference?"

"Maybe not. That's a hard question to decide. Only thing is the estate ought to be settled. Ben could be in a bad way somewhere and needing his share of the money. Hate to think that while I was off having it easy, he was in want."

"I thought, from what you told me about him, that he'd likely be able to take care of himself."

"Probably is, far as I know. And he has been in the past, but things can happen—and I've lost track of him. Could mean he's in trouble."

Glory sighed. "There's so much here, Shawn—for both of us, but it won't mean anything to me unless you share it."

"Appreciate that—but I was careful to make it clear to you where I stood."

"I know, but I keep hoping—"

"Don't. Just won't work out. Right now, it's important you get your mine to going—maybe do some thinking about Kruger."

"Horst? Why?"

"The man's lost himself to you. Sticks out all over him."

She stared at him, lips parted in surprise. "Why, I never thought—"

"That's how it is, sometimes. He'd make you a good partner—and husband."

Abruptly, Glory was cool. "I can pick my own husband," she said quietly.

Starbuck grinned. "Not doing any choosing for you, only calling your attention to something you're missing."

She made no comment. The mules jogged on at a slow trot, their load pulling easily over the fairly level stretch of road they were now traveling. Overhead, the sky was a clear blue, unmarked except for a scatter of small clouds to the east and a pair of vultures soaring in a wide circle above a distant mountain.

"Why did your brother leave home?"

Her question, coming minutes later, was unexpected, and Shawn, attention on a spur of dense brush and trees jutting out from the river a mile or so ahead, was slow in replying.

"Was a row he had with Pa over some chores he forgot to do. Sounds like a little thing now, but it had sort of built up. Pa was strict, expected us to do what we were told—and no arguing about it."

"Having a home—a ma and a pa and a brother—must have been nice."

"Was. Our farm was a good one. Could grow about anything we wanted, and there was always plenty of everything. Had good times, too, Ben and me, and we didn't miss much. My mother saw to it that we got good schooling; Pa taught us all the rest of the things we needed to know. He was a little hard on us at times, but it was worth it . . . Can see that now."

"I can't think of many good things to remember about my life," Glory said wistfully. "We did little else except move from one place to another until Wickenburg. I hardly knew what a school was before then, but Mama tried to make up for it. I sometimes feel that I never was a child, that I was always grown."

"We get your mine to paying off the way everybody seems to think it will, you can make up for a lot of that."

"Everything except the lost years. Not all the silver in the world can buy them back or wipe out the bad things that happened."

"We all have a few things we need to forget," Starbuck said gently, "and that's the best thing to do, forget them. Practical, too, because you can't go back to the beginning and start over."

"It's what I'm hoping to do, Shawn, and I wanted you to help me—"

He locked the rifle between his knees and, reaching up, brushed the sweat from his face. He was uncomfortable with the conversation, wished again that Kruger or one of the Mexicans could have made the trip with him.

"That's something else we have to learn to live with—can't always have things our way."

Glory slapped the reins smartly against the hindquarters of the mules, urging them to a faster pace. They had slowed almost to a walk.

"How much farther is it to that mill?" she asked briskly, as if shaking off her dark thoughts and deciding to concentrate on the business at hand.

"Couple of miles or so past those trees ahead," Starbuck said, pointing to the spur of tangled growth and weedy rocks they were approaching. "If you're tired of driving, I'll spell you."

"I'm all right," she snapped, and again laid the leathers on the mules' backs with a quick flip.

The animals quickened to a trot. Starbuck, rifle again across his knees, studied the rough, broken area they were entering with narrowed eyes. It was the one section along the river road that had troubled him the day when he'd made his survey of the route. If there were to be an attempt to hijack the load of ore, it likely would take place in that ragged, desolate area.

It came when they were little more than halfway across the narrow band. Four riders, bandanna masks covering their faces, spurted suddenly from the brush, began converging on the wagon, two from each side.

Starbuck came to attention instantly, and as the rider nearest lifted his pistol and fired, he leaned forward, shoved the girl down between the wagon's dashboard and the seat.

"Anything happens to me," he said grimly as he levered a cartridge into the rifle's chamber, "don't stop. Keep driving this road—it'll take you to the mill . . . Now, get those mules moving!"

SIXTEEN

Glory lashed out with her whip. Starbuck braced himself. The team lunged into the harness, the wagon jerked, and began to rock and sway as it picked up speed over the uneven ground. Crouched, Shawn took quick aim at the rider closest to them, triggered a shot.

The outlaw jolted as the bullet drove into him. He buckled forward, clutched at the saddlehorn to keep from falling. His partners, firing only sporadically and apparently caught unawares by unexpected opposition, began to fall back in the face of the steady stream of lead from Starbuck's rifle. He was having no luck scoring again; the combination of an unfamiliar weapon and the lurching vehicle made accuracy impossible.

The long gun clicked on an empty chamber. There were more cartridges in a sack he'd thrust into his pocket, but there was no time to reload. Three of the outlaws, over their surprise apparently, had curved in behind them and were now coming on fast. The fourth, a limp shape on his horse, had halted at the side of the road.

Drawing his forty-five, Shawn opened up with the heavy pistol. Despite the erratic motion of the wagon, now out of the brushy spur and racing downgrade, his shooting was more effective.

Through the dust haze, he saw one of the riders flinch. He could not tell if the man was hit or if it had been a near miss. Regardless, the outlaw reined in. Immediately, the two remaining riders slowed, and then all three once again pulled away, and shortly all were hidden by the drifting gray pall.

Starbuck turned to the girl. She was on her knees, hunched between the seat and the dashboard where he had pushed her. Somewhere back up the way, she had dropped the whip and was now struggling to control the madly running mules in full flight for Charleston, only a half mile or so in the distance.

Pulling her back to an upright position beside him, Shawn took the reins from her cramped fingers and began to slow the team. A streak of bright red tracing across the near mule's croup showed where a bullet had found its mark. It appeared not to be a serious wound; it likely had served only as a spur to the animal's speed.

"Have they gone?" Glory asked, looking around. Her face was white, and there was a tightness to her mouth.

Starbuck nodded. "We're all right now. That's the mill up ahead."

Sighing deeply, she relaxed, resting quietly as he brought the team under control. And then she glanced up at him.

"I know you worried about something like

this happening. I—I guess I just didn't believe it could."

Starbuck barely heard her words. He was thinking back to the visit T. J. Yorkan had made to the mine, suspicion mounting steadily within him.

"That lawyer—Yorkan—he ask you when we'd be taking the first load of ore to the mill when he dropped by the other day?"

Glory pulled herself upright. "Why, yes, he did. Just sort of came up in the conversation."

"You tell him it would be today?"

"Yes, I did," the girl replied, frowning. "Was there anything wrong in—" She broke off suddenly, eyes going wide. "You don't think he had something to do with this—with those outlaws!"

"Be to his advantage to have you fail. Don't want to forget that."

"I know—but Mr. Yorkan! He's a big man, well known, and he's probably already rich. He doesn't look like somebody that would stoop to robbery—"

"Can't go by looks—and there's something about money that makes a man who has a lot of it want more sometimes."

She fell silent as they swung in toward the cluster of structures that made up the stamp mill. As the team slowed she said, "Are you going to accuse him of it?"

"Not that sure of things. Be a waste of time,

anyway. He'd deny it. One thing sure, whoever it is will have that bunch try again."

"They could've been just some outlaws. Horst said there were plenty of them around here."

"A holdup's more likely to happen after the ore has been turned into silver bullion. Not saying they won't grab a few tons of rich ore if they get the chance, but that means they've got to get it processed at some mill, and that could lead to questions . . . Guess we're here."

Starbuck pulled the wagon to a halt beside a small office. A steady thumping sound was coming from the mill itself, and as he rose to quiet the mules, a man in dusty overalls came out of the board shack to meet them.

Squat, husky, red-bearded, he threw a critical look at the load in the wagon and nodded. "Name's Baxter. I'm the superintendent. Ain't much ore there."

Shawn introduced Glory and himself. "That's how it'll be until we can get things going. There a chance you can run this load through right away?"

Baxter glanced over his shoulder to where one of the large ore wagons was backed up to a hopper. "In a hurry, eh? Yeah, expect I could handle it special."

"That's what we'd like. Important that we see where we stand and then get back and load up again."

Baxter shrugged noncommittally, shifted his attention to the injured mule. "Thought I heard some shooting a while back, but there's so danged much racket around here I wasn't sure . . . You run into trouble?"

"Outlaws—four of them. Tried to stop us . . . There a livery stable here where I can get the mule doctored?"

"Old man Jenks's place—across the bridge and to the left. Pull your rig over there by that other'n and unhitch your team. We'll do the rest. The young lady can wait in my office if she's of a mind."

Leaving Glory with Baxter, Starbuck drove the wagon to the designated spot, and then, unhooking the traces and releasing the tongue, he slung the trailing harness over the mule's backs, and riding one, crossed the stream and sought out Jenks.

The wound proved to be only minor. The combination blacksmith and stable owner, a soft-spoken, smiling little man with a singed beard, dressed it by first dousing the raw furrow with a liniment antiseptic, which set the animal to bucking and plunging wildly. When that was over, and the mule was again quiet, he smeared the injury with thick grease and pronounced the treatment complete.

Shawn returned to the mill office and rejoined Glory. It would be some time yet, she said, but she wanted to wait for the final results. Shawn agreed; they should know what the bullion yield of the ore was before returning to the mine and thus be able to figure how much more they would need to haul in order to meet Yorkan's deadline.

But he was taut and restless from the encounter with the outlaws, and he could not see them just sitting around the mill, passing time.

"There's a restaurant across the way," he said, reaching for her hand. "Let's go there, have ourselves a bite of dinner. Afterwards, we can get a rig from the livery stable, have a look around if you'd like."

Glory's features flushed with pleasure. "I would—very much," she replied, rising.

It was late in the day when they pulled out of Charleston. Glory had settled with the mine superintendent, getting a receipt for the bullion, which would be honored by the stage company office in Tombstone.

"That's how most of the mining companies are handling it," she explained. "Baxter said it wasn't safe for anyone to be on the road with silver right now, so they ship it under heavy guard to Bisbee and put it in a bank there for us. I can draw whatever I want against my deposit."

It was a good arrangement, and Starbuck was relieved to know the bullion would be secure. "How much silver did you come out with?"

Some of the shine faded from her eyes. "Only about four thousand dollars' worth. It figured around eighteen hundred a ton, they said . . . I thought—hoped—it would be more."

"Still plenty good," Shawn said. "Means we'll need to haul in two more loads to meet Yorkan's note—leastwise that's all we'll need if the ore stays as rich as this batch."

Glory frowned. "Didn't somebody say that it was worth four thousand dollars a ton? Seems like I remember—"

"Was Kruger, that day in Trimm's office. I forgot about that," Starbuck said, raising his voice to be heard above the rattling of the empty wagon. "We'll ask him about it when we get back. Don't know anything about mining, but that seems a big difference between the samples your pa took in to be assayed and what they're digging out now."

"Could the mine be playing out before we even get started—be just a pocket, I think it's called?"

"Always a chance," Starbuck answered. "One thing I'm sure of—"

She glanced at him. "What's that?"

"This time, nobody's to know when we'll make the haul—only you, Kruger, and me. Might not be a bad idea to hire on a couple of outriders."

"Outriders?"

"Guards. With only ten days left before that

note's due, we can't risk being hijacked—or any other delay."

She was quiet for a time, then, "Do you still think it's Yorkan behind it?"

"He's the one who'll benefit the most if you don't make the deadline. Whoever, we upset their plans this time. I don't think they expected us to be on the lookout and ready. Next time it'll be them that's ready, and it won't be so easy to turn them back."

"If it's the same bunch," the girl said. "Do you think we can hire extra guards?"

"Can try when I'm in Tombstone tonight," Starbuck said as they swung toward the canyon. "Figured I'd ride in and do some more asking about my brother."

Glory murmured her understanding in a listless voice. She would like to go with him, he knew, but the roaring streets of the town were no place for a woman after dark unless she were closely escorted, and he would have no time for that.

SEVENTEEN

A third motive lay behind Starbuck's intention to visit Tombstone that night, one that could possibly afford him a clue as to who it was behind the attempt to ruin, even murder, Glory Cannon. While the girl was still unconvinced, the would-be hijackers were no more than vagrant outlaws looking for an easy take, he could not make himself believe it.

He was certain they had been hired to set up an ambush and prevent the delivery of the ore to the mill, and if luck was with him, he just might learn who the four men were since he now had something to go on. Heading first for Melly Jones's place, since he was more or less known there, he singled out one of the bartenders.

Ordering a drink, he said, "Was over along the San Pedro today. Was a shooting—not sure if there was a killing or not. You hear anything about it—maybe who it was?"

The counterman scratched at the stubble on his jaw. "You a-feared it might've been that brother you're hunting?"

Such hadn't been in Starbuck's mind, but he said, "Make it a rule to look into about everything—"

"Well, I didn't hear nothing. Don't expect to.

Somebody gets hisself killed around here, nobody hardly looks around to see who he is. And getting shot just ain't nothing at all . . . Good thing you dropped by, howsoever."

"That so?"

"Yeah. Parker, that jasper you tangled with in here the other day—he was bad mouthing you something fierce after you left. Says he's going to square up with you for batting him around—and he'll do it, one way or another."

Shawn tossed off his whiskey, then came about and glanced around. There were perhaps two dozen patrons in the saloon. Parker was not one of them.

"Just wanted you to know," the bartender said.

"Obliged to you," Starbuck replied, moving on. "I'll keep my eyes peeled."

What the barman had said about the shooting proved to be the same story in all of the other establishments that he visited; no one had heard of it—and no one knew a Ben Starbuck or Damon Friend, and there was no one interested in hiring on as a wagon guard. Those who weren't working already had no intentions of taking a job—money was too easy to come by just by hanging around the town. And riding shotgun down the San Pedro valley? Hell, that was about as quick a way as a man could figure to get himself planted on Boot Hill.

Thus, the hours spent in Tombstone went for nothing, unless he could count the negative replies concerning his brother. Glory accepted his report on the failure to hire extra guards with little reaction, seemingly confident that he alone was sufficient protection, and two days later, after a feverishly working Horst Kruger and his helpers had finished loading the wagon for the second time, she was on the seat and waiting to pull out, apparently oblivious to any possible danger.

Starbuck viewed the matter in a different light. The first attempt to sidetrack the shipment of ore had failed, but it could be a different story this time unless he took every precaution. That he fully intended to do, and along with that determination, he would put a stop to such efforts regardless of who was at the bottom of it—hijackers looking to make easy money or hired outlaws sent to accomplish a purpose.

It would be necessary to make the small hauls even after Yorkan's note was satisfied, since they must then work to develop the mine and put it on a paying basis. Cash would be required for equipment, supplies, wages, and the like, and such could be derived only from ore delivered to the mill—and Starbuck was no man to put up with a continuing threat of interference.

"Taking my horse this time," he said, tying the sorrel on behind the wagon and climbing onto the seat beside the girl. "We run into trouble again, he'll come in handy."

"How?" the girl asked, with an offhand wave at Horst Kruger, silently looking on from the entrance to the mine shaft.

"Aim to go after them. I get my hands on a live one, I'll find out who's behind this hold-up business," he replied as the mules moved out.

"Still wonder if they aren't just robbers—"

"Be all right with me. Main thing is I've got to do something about it."

"There's still three of them if it's the same bunch—and there could be more this time . . . You'll be taking a big chance, Shawn."

"What you're paying me for," he said as the wagon began to gather speed on the slight grade. "We'll work it the same as the other day. They show up, you head for Charleston fast as those mules can go—just give me time to get back to my horse."

Glory signified her understanding and shrugged wearily. "Is this the way it's going to be all the time—worrying about getting every load of ore to the mill?"

"What I'm going to try and change."

"I'm starting to wonder if the mine's worth it. There's too much risk."

"If we're lucky, I'll put them out of business today," he said. "Kruger have anything to say about this load of ore—whether it was better than the first one or not?"

"I talked to him about it a little. He didn't give me much of an answer, just sort of acted like he was doing his job the best he could."

"Can't blame him if the ore's poor, that's for sure, but we're needing some high-grade if you're to meet that note on time . . . Yorkan didn't happen to come by again, did he?"

Glory shook her head. "No, I haven't seen him since the day he brought that New York man by."

"Good. Means only you, Kruger, and I know about this shipment."

"That's all unless there's somebody watching us."

"Good chance of that, too," Starbuck admitted and gave the girl a sideward glance.

She had changed in these past few days—was now quiet, withdrawn, with all of her earlier enthusiasm absent. It was as if the good fortune that had befallen her no longer held any appeal, but he supposed that was because she had grown weary of the problems she was being forced to face. Hopefully by dark that day, he would be able to ease some of the strain on her.

They rolled on in the warm fall afternoon, while the line of golden-leafed cottonwoods along the river gradually drew nearer and was finally alongside the road. Starbuck began to search the country ahead. The spur of brush, rocks, and stunted trees where the outlaws had hidden previously was still well to the south, but he studied it carefully; if the ragged brakes again concealed an ambush, he wanted to know it.

He saw no signs of such, however, and the thought began to grow in his mind as they drew nearer that Glory could be right, that the four outlaws who had jumped them were no more than that—ordinary road agents and not likely to try their luck a second time after the reception they encountered. He hoped such would prove to be the fact; if so, they had nothing to fear from T. J. Yorkan.

But that would not clear up the killing of Ira Cannon or the attempt on Glory's life, Starbuck realized in that next moment. And if it wasn't the lawyer, it was someone else.

He stiffened suddenly. The bright glint of sunlight striking metal had caught his eye . . . Someone with a gun was waiting in the rocks to the east of the road. There was still a long mile to the jutting spur of brush, and if it was an ambush, the outlaws, either the same ones or another bunch, had chosen a different point from which to spring an attack.

"Up there—on that hill," he said, drawing the girl's attention to the isolated mound. "Somebody's there. Want you to be ready if it turns out to be hijackers."

Glory nodded, fixed her eyes on the weedy

rocks. "Shawn—you'll take care," she said slowly as the tightness began to show around her lips.

"Can bet on it," he replied, pulling his pistol and checking its loads. Then smiling at her, he added, "I'll get back to the sorrel—just in case."

"Hadn't I better stop?"

"No, I'll crawl over the load, maybe do it without them noticing," he said, and keeping low, turned about and pulled himself over the seat onto the tarp-covered ore.

Halfway to the rear of the wagon bed, he paused. "I'm going after them," he reminded her. "When you reach Charleston, stay there. I'll come for you soon as I get my rope on one of them. May be late, but I'll come, so wait."

"All right," Glory said, her words barely audible above the creaking and grumbling of the wagon.

Shawn continued, worming his way along the canvas cover until he reached the vehicle's tail-gate. Rolling to his side, he threw his glance to the rocks. The mound was only a quarter mile in the distance. Freeing the gelding's reins, Starbuck drew his legs up beneath him, eyes again on the ragged hill. He doubted anyone there could see him, for the flared sides of the wagon bed closed him off from view fairly well, but if the outlaws were watching closely, they would have become aware there was now but one person on the seat and perhaps wonder at the change that had been made.

The mules drew abreast the mound. No one appeared. Glory looked back at him questioningly. He shook his head. There was someone there, hiding in the brush and rocks; he had not imagined the flash of light. They could be waiting for—

Gunshots broke out suddenly. Dust spurted up a distance from the edge of the road, well short of the wagon. The raiders were there, all right, but they had misjudged the range of their weapons and opened up too soon.

"Get out of here!" he shouted and threw himself off the back of the wagon.

Shawn hit the ground with solid force as the team plunged ahead, went off balance and down, all the while hanging tight to the sorrel's leathers. Unhurt, he bounded upright, and one hand going swiftly to his pistol, he caught the saddlehorn with the other and vaulted onto the shying horse.

Yanking savagely on the bit, he cut the big gelding about and spurred toward the three riders streaming down the grade. A tight grin pulled back his lips. They were the same men as before—the same gang minus the one he'd put a bullet into. They were not just ordinary outlaws but riders sent by someone to prevent the delivery of the ore.

Starbuck flung a glance at the wagon. It was

whirling off down the dusty tracks, moving fast. He need not worry about Glory Cannon. Bringing his attention back to the outlaws, he snapped a shot at the one in the lead. All slowed, seemingly noticing him for the first time. Bent low on the sorrel, he fired again.

Horst Kruger stood quietly listening to the clatter of the departing ore wagon, and then, when he could no longer hear it, he wheeled slowly, and his square face set in thoughtful lines, crossed to the fire where the pot of breakfast coffee still simmered over the coals. Filling one of the tin cups, he sat down on a nearby nail keg.

Inside the mine, the two laborers had resumed work, digging away at the south wall. They still could not understand why he had instructed them to ignore the high-grade ore on the opposite side and to confine their efforts to removing the poor stuff for shipment to the stamp mill, but by a mixture of pidgin English and halting Spanish, he had convinced them that it was what he wanted and, since he was the *patron*, they followed his orders.

But something was wrong. There had evidently been a change of plans, and his partner had neglected, for some reason, to notify him.

There had been nothing said about hijacking or interfering with the hauling of ore; the scheme called for him to mine only the low-grade stuff, convince Glory Cannon by so doing that her claim was worth little and would be too costly to work, that it would only be good common sense to give it up.

Now, that plan had apparently been scrapped for some reason, a good one no doubt, and matters were taking a course of violence. Kruger didn't like that. He'd said at the start he wouldn't stand for any harm coming to the girl, and he still meant it.

Horst, in his slow, methodical way, had mulled the situation about in his mind ever since Glory and Starbuck had returned from that first haul to the mill and he'd learned of the attack. The wound sustained by one of the mules and the several bullets buried in the thick planks of the wagon bed were proof enough that the raiders meant business, had failed in what they were sent to do only because of Starbuck.

And they weren't just outlaws, as Glory seemed to think; from the description he was able to get from her, he recognized them as Tip Yarbro, Billy Riddle, Nate Bowie, and Harley Gates. Gates had been the one that Starbuck shot. All worked for the man he was in partnership with, doing whatever sort of job he wanted done.

Things had gotten out of hand, somehow, and now that Glory and Starbuck weren't hovering around, pressing him to get out enough ore for a haul, he'd go into town, demand that Yarbro and the others be called off, and the original plan be allowed to proceed. If something had occurred that called for the use of guns, then he was through—*finished*—and he'd back out of the deal, fortune or not.

Kruger tossed away the last of the coffee. Rising, he glanced at the sun. Best he get started. It was a long walk to Tombstone.

EIGHTEEN

The outlaws, forgetting Glory Cannon and the ore wagon, swung toward Starbuck. Crouched low on the saddle, Shawn triggered two more shots at them. All three began to return his fire, but their horses were fighting the bit and shying nervously in the face of the charging sorrel. Suddenly, the rider to the left of the party, a slightly built individual wearing a faded red-and-black-checked shirt, wheeled, spurred for the safety of the rocks. His two friends hesitated briefly, and then they too cut about sharply and streaked for cover.

Starbuck, reloading as the gelding pounded up the grade, kept his eyes fixed on a shoulder of sandstone behind which the outlaws had disappeared. There was no doubt now that someone had hired the men to waylay Glory and the shipment of silver ore, and in his own mind, he believed it could be no one else but T. J. Yorkan—but he still had no proof . . . He'd take care of that little detail now, however, he thought grimly; all he needed to do was get his hands on one of the outlaws, make him talk.

He gained the bulge of rock and slowed. They'd be waiting for him in the brush on the opposite side of the formation, he reckoned, and the moment he rode into sight, they'd meet him

NINETEEN

It was full dark when Starbuck, riding the gelding hard, swung out of the valley and into the canyon where Ira Cannon had made his strike. Fear jolted him solidly as he rushed by the corral where the mules were kept. Neither the animals nor the wagon were there.

The sorrel pounded his way to the top of the trail and broke out onto the plateau fronting the shaft. A lantern hung near the entrance, and the two Mexicans were hunkered near the low fire, chewing on strips of jerky.

"Where's Kruger?" he shouted, pulling to a halt.

The younger of the pair got to his feet. "He has gone, *señor*," he said haltingly.

"Gone where?" Shawn demanded impatiently.

The man shrugged. "We are work inside the mine and do not know. To the town, I would believe."

Starbuck frowned. The engineer had apparently left during daylight hours despite an awareness that getting out sufficient ore for shipment to the mill as fast as possible was critically necessary; just why he would neglect his responsibilities was difficult to understand. But such was a matter to be looked into later, he realized, staring off into the valley brightening now under a rising moon.

A coldness gripped him. Glory was down there somewhere, prisoner or victim of outlaws or Apaches. At once, he swung the sorrel about and started down the trail. He had but one choice—get back down to the road, search for the tracks of the wagon and team.

Finding them would be a matter of luck pushed to its limit, he had to admit as he reached the mouth of the wash and dropped back to the floor of the valley; while the stars and moon were flooding the slopes and flats with a pale silver glow, actual trailing would be a tough job.

His best chances would be to return to the mill and there endeavor to pick up Glory's tracks when she drove off on the return trip. The wheels of the wagon had wide iron tires, and their impressions in places would be plainly visible. In daylight, the task would be fairly simple, but at night it was an entirely different situation. It made no difference, nevertheless; he had to find Glory Cannon, and taking the course they followed going to and from Charleston, he rode hard.

Except for lights showing in a few windows, the little mill town was in darkness when he arrived. Making a hurried circuit of the settlement to assure himself the wagon and team of mules were not there, he doubled back to the road that led up to the mill itself. Halting at the point where the river trail turned onto it, he dropped to the ground, made a careful examination of the many flat ribbon-like imprints left by wheels.

They were plentiful, and he moved on, a relentless urgency pressing him, leading the sorrel, head bent forward and eyes on the grassy soil as he sought to separate the most recent tracks from the others.

In a small strip of gritty sand, he had his first success. Seeing what appeared to be prints overlaying others, he squatted, tested the sharp edge of the impressions with a fingertip. The sand was loose and crumbled readily. Satisfaction stirred him as he drew himself upright. This much he knew—Glory had started back for the mine, had taken no other route.

Still leading his horse, Starbuck moved along the road, striving to keep the prints before him while all the time watching for any indication of the wagon's turning off. In only a short distance, he realized he faced a hopeless chore; all prints faded when he came to a broad flinty slope across which the trail angled.

He halted there, staring off toward the dark stand of brush and rock that had served the outlaws as a point for their ambush. He had seen nothing of the wagon on the way down, and now his one hope of tracking the vehicle was lost in a wide expanse of hard ground. As well turn his efforts to that brake like section, see if by chance the girl's kidnappers had taken her and the wagon there for hiding.

Mounting the sorrel, he veered from the now indiscernible road and walked the gelding quietly toward the first line of brush looming up before him like a shadowy wall in the night. Gaining it, he again stopped, a faint sound coming from the head-high growth somewhere ahead. Motionless, worry plucking at him continually, he listened.

The noise did not come again. He moved on, still walking the gelding, but left hand now resting on the butt of the forty-five thonged to his leg. Once more, he drew up. The sound had reached him for the second time—a faint jingling of metal.

Instantly, he was off the saddle, and crouched low, he began to work his way through the rocks and brush. Shortly, he climbed a low rise, hunched lower. A dozen strides away, showing clearly in the soft light, was the team and wagon.

For several long minutes, he studied the small clearing, probing its fringe carefully until he was positive the parked vehicle was no trap, and then moved in close.

He could tell little of what might have happened. There were no signs of a struggle, only the empty wagon and the weary mules standing, head down in the half dark. It had been the rattle of harness metal as one of the animals stirred that caught his attention.

Nor could he determine anything from footprints around the vehicle or turn up any hoof marks that would reveal how many were in the party that had kidnapped Glory and whether they were outlaws or Indians. He was at a dead end until it became light enough for him to begin a thorough inspection of the ground.

Meanwhile, he could only wait, but the makeup of Shawn Starbuck would not permit him to do so idly; he'd occupy those worry-filled, dragging hours by searching the surrounding area of brush and rock on the possibility that those who had the girl were holding her nearby, also delaying until daylight. He had little faith in such being the fact, but picketing the sorrel to one of the wagon's wheels, he nevertheless began a systematic examination.

TWENTY-ONE

"What're we going to do about Harley? We giving him his share?"

It was the outlaw in the faded, checked shirt. He now had a bandage about his neck, proof that one of Shawn's bullets had found its mark, if only a graze, that previous day. But it had been enough to turn him and his friends aside, send them scurrying for Tombstone.

Crouched in the brush, Starbuck strained to see inside the shack. Glory had to be in there—unless he was wrong about everything. He brought his attention back to the outlaws. The coffee had come to a boil, and a chunky, thick-armed man was pouring the black, steaming liquid into tin cups.

"He ain't here, he don't get," the third member of the party said dryly. He was small, narrow-faced, and had a knife scar tracing from ear to chin on his left cheek.

"Ain't no fault of ours he let hisself get all shot up by that jasper. Ain't that the way you see it, Billy?"

Billy was the man in the checked shirt. "Reckon so, but it sure seems he ought to get something. Been riding with us quite a spell."

"We forget him, we'll only have to split three

ways," scar-face pointed out. "Now, that sounds mighty good to me. How about you, Nate?"

Nate, his own cup filled, set the pot back over the fire, took a cautious sip of the hot coffee. "I'm with you, Tip. If Billy wants to fork over some of his share to Harley, I reckon it's up to him. Aim to keep mine, every damn cent 'cause we sure'n hell have earned it . . . Wonder if that gal'd like some of this here coffee?"

"She don't like nothing—much," Tip grumbled. "Tried cozying up to her last night, and all I got was a kick on the shins. Can go without, far as I'm concerned."

Billy laughed, glanced toward the cabin. "She's a ring-tailed, stem-winder, all right!"

Starbuck silently moved a few paces to his left, brought himself into position for a more direct look into the shack. He breathed easier. Glory Cannon was there. Hands tied behind her, ankles bound, she sat on the dirt floor in a back corner. She appeared to be unharmed.

Earlier, Shawn had wondered if the girl had fallen into the hands of the same outlaws or if he was up against an entirely different bunch. He had assumed the former to be true. Now that it was definite, he realized he had been tricked—accidentally, no doubt, but still tricked.

The three men, aware he had trailed them to Tombstone, and undoubtedly seeing him searching the town for them, had returned at once to the mill, where they knew Glory would be waiting. More than likely, they had first reported to whoever it was that wanted the girl out of the way, and it was on his—or their—order that they acted. Glory had made it easier for them by starting back to the mill alone.

Drawing up his legs beneath him, Starbuck set himself to confront the outlaws. It should be no chore. He'd simply step into the open, and gun leveled, order them to throw up their hands. He'd learned they were not among the bravest of men, and none was likely to show any resistance.

"Pay day ought to be getting here," Tip said, swallowing the last of his coffee and setting the cup on the rocks encircling the fire. "Deal was he'd be here by noon."

Starbuck paused, interest quickening within him. The outlaw could only mean that the man behind it all, the one who wanted Ira Cannon's mine so badly he would hesitate at nothing, was due to appear. Evidently, he was bringing cash to pay off the outlaws for their services.

He threw a hasty look at the girl. She would be all right; uncomfortable, no doubt, but remaining in the cabin a few minutes longer would make little difference—and it was important, for her sake, that he know for certain who her enemy was.

Billy rose, stretched, and yawned noisily. "Reckon I'll take a gander, see if I can spot him," he said, and turning, walked toward a mound of rocks a short distance from the cabin.

Tip got to his feet, strolled to the entrance of the shack, and glanced in. Glory did not raise her eyes. The outlaw said something to her in a low voice, which brought no response, and grinning, he came about, moved off after Billy.

Nate continued to squat by the fire, taking short sips from his cup. After a time, he reached for the pot, refilled the tin container. He came erect then, crossed to where the horses stood. Halting beside one, he dug a near-empty bottle of whiskey from the saddlebags and laced the coffee liberally with the liquor. On beyond him in the rocks, a ground squirrel barked sharply.

"He's a-coming!"

Billy shouted the word back to his friends. Tip had halted midway to the mound, was rolling a cigarette. Nate, sucking at his cup, grunted, returned to the fire, and dropped to his heels.

"About time," he said. "Got a hell of a long ride ahead of us yet before we're done."

Starbuck swiped at his face. The brush was swarming with small black gnats, and they hovered around him in a shifting, irritating cloud. Heat, too, had mounted until he was now clothed with sweat.

"You reckon we could make him kick in with a little something for Harley?" Billy wondered as he sauntered back into camp. "Sure wouldn't miss a couple a hundred—coming out with all he figures to get."

"Be wasting your breath," Tip said. "He ain't parting with a nickel more'n he has to."

"Well, I aim to ask, anyway—"

"What the hell's eating you, Billy?" Nate demanded impatiently. "You take on Harley to raise? Was he you and you him, he wouldn't be stewing about it."

"Ain't so sure of that. Harley's a pretty square shooter."

" 'Cepting when it comes down to cold cash," Tip said. "That there's something else. He wouldn't give you a copper if it had to come out of his pocket."

Billy shrugged, hunched beside the fire again, and began to toss bits of twigs and dry branches into the dwindling flames.

"Maybe you're right," he said after a time. "I reckon we ain't apt to see him again no how—not if we ain't figuring to go back to Tombstone."

"Was part of the deal that we're to move on, stay out of sight for a year."

"What's he wanting that for? Scared we might spill the beans?"

"Expect so. He's a mighty careful gent."

"He's got a reason to be—putting a bullet in that old prospector, then euchring the gal out of her mine."

with a hail of bullets. They'd not find him that easy.

Pulling up, Starbuck dropped quietly to the ground and, gun in hand, worked his way through the brush and rocks to the front of the monolith. Then, flat on his belly, he crawled along the base of the formation until he gained its opposite side. Surprise brought him to his feet. A quarter mile down the valley, the outlaws were only vague figures in the dust as they rode hard in the direction of Tombstone.

Cursing, Shawn wheeled, doubled back to where he'd left the sorrel. Swinging onto the saddle, he circled the rock and, reaching the smooth ground a short distance beyond, roweled the big gelding into a galloping pursuit.

He had fleeting glimpses of the three men as they broke in and out of brush patches and clumps of trees, or appeared briefly on the crest of higher rises, but soon the gray dust haze that enveloped Tombstone came into view, and he realized the outlaws would reach the settlement well ahead of him. Shawn swore again; once they gained its teeming confusion, finding them would be next to impossible.

He must overtake them, and crouching lower, he called on the sorrel for more speed. The gelding responded, his long, powerful legs flashing out, eating up distance at an amazing rate—but it was a lost cause.

As Starbuck topped out the final hill and reached the flat, he saw the riders moving into the scatter of tents at the extreme edge of the town. Moments later, they came to the lower end of a street, turned into it, and became lost to sight.

Easing up on the sorrel, Shawn rode on. His hope of following and catching up with the outlaws was lost, but he was not giving it up. He could still search for them. He'd gotten a good look at all three this time, and there was a chance the one in the checked shirt was wounded; his earlier actions had indicated that a bullet had either struck him or else had come so close that he was unnerved enough to turn him back.

He drew nearer, a stir of satisfaction moving through him. He was entering the town at a familiar point; the first building in the line was Melly Jones's saloon. Pulling the sorrel to a stop at the hitch rack, he dismounted hurriedly, wrapped the leathers about the crossbar, and headed for the adjacent street, which led to the center of the settlement.

A half-dozen men lounged along the wall of the saloon, soaking up sunshine as he rounded the corner of the structure. Intent on his purpose, eyes reaching ahead, hoping for a glimpse of the outlaws, he gave no thought to them. And then a vaguely familiar voice, heavy with sarcasm, drew his attention.

"Well, if it ain't our highfalutin boxing man!"

Starbuck slowed, swung his attention to the speaker . . . Parker, the drunk he'd had a little trouble with in Jones's saloon. Shawn nodded coldly, continued on.

At once, the group of grinning men with Parker edged out onto the dusty walk and blocked his path. He realized they had seen him approaching and, at Parker's suggestion, most likely, had planned a reception.

"Get the hell out of my way," he snapped, resuming stride. "You got something to say to me, save it till later!"

Abruptly, the gang closed in. Anger flaring, Shawn struck out with both fists. Instantly, hands caught at his arms, pinned them to his sides, dragged him off balance. A blow came out of nowhere, nailed him flush on the jaw. Stunned, he felt himself being half-carried, half-dragged behind the saloon.

"Hold him up, boys—"

It was Parker's voice. Starbuck shook his head, struggling to clear away the haze floating before his eyes. The men had formed a ring around him. Two were supporting him, hands under his armpits. Parker faced him, an oily shine on his skin, a hard grin on his thick lips.

"Been waiting for this," he said, and swung a balled fist.

Starbuck, senses slowly recovering, reacted instinctively. He rocked to one side, avoided the man's clumsy blow, and, raising a knee, drove it into Parker's belly. Suddenly free of the hands bolstering him, Shawn spun away.

Parker, mouth gaping, eyes rolling wildly, staggered back. Starbuck surged toward him, grimly determined to end the scuffle and continue his search for the outlaws before too much time elapsed. He felt a blow across the shoulders and stumbled uncertainly. An outstretched leg blocked his foot. He tripped, went down full length into the dust.

He started to roll aside, pull himself upright, but took another shocking blow on the back of his neck. A boot drove into his ribs, sent a spurt of pain through him. He tried again to roll clear, succeeded, bounded to his feet, anger now a soaring, raging force within him. He wheeled, smashed a fist into the sweaty face of the nearest man, pivoted to meet another. In that same moment, something crashed down onto his head. His brain reeled, and a surge of blackness swept over him. Through dimming eyes, he saw the ground rising to meet him.

Starbuck roused slowly. He was lying against the wall of a small shed a short distance from the saloon. He'd been dragged there by Parker and his friends, he supposed, after they'd knocked him senseless. How long he had lain there was problematical—likely a quarter hour, no more than twice that, he guessed as he drew himself painfully upright.

His ribs ached where he'd been kicked, his shoulders were sore, and there was a dull pain in the back of his head, but other than that, he seemed to have sustained no serious injuries. Bracing himself with a hand against the wall of the shed, he glanced about. The street up which he had started was a dozen yards away. He could see no sign of Parker and his followers.

The outlaws . . . Remembrance came abruptly to him. Unsteady, he moved toward the street, left hand unconsciously dropping to the pistol on his hip, making certain that it was in the holster. The three men would have had ample time to lose themselves in Tombstone's crowds by then, even find an effective hiding place if they felt it necessary.

Cursing Parker, Shawn reached the dusty lane, turned into it, and, ignoring the stiffness restricting his steps, hurried as best he could to the intersection. Reaching Allen, he swung onto it and began a tour of the settlement. Finally, a time later, he halted, shook his head in resignation. As well forget it. He would never be able to locate the outlaws—and there wasn't enough time to search through all of the saloons and other possible hiding places, even if it were practical.

Coming about, he doubled back to Melly Jones's and the rack where he'd left the sorrel.

He should be returning to Charleston and Glory, anyway; she would be ready for the return trip to the mine by that hour, and his failure to appear would set her to worrying.

But he could not resist the impulse to stop at the saloon, and anger again whipping through him, he stepped into the open doorway. Halted just inside, he swept the dozen or so patrons with his pushing glance. A few of those present looked familiar, could have been in the party siding Parker, but the man himself was not to be seen. Nodding curtly to those who had turned to face him, he dropped back to the walk and crossed to the waiting sorrel. Mounting, he cut the gelding about and spurred him into a fast lope for Charleston. He and Parker would meet again one day. He'd see to that.

It wasn't far short of sundown when Starbuck rode up to the office of mill super Baxter. As he pulled to a stop, a frown covered his brow, and a quick worry filled his mind; there was no sign of the ore wagon and team.

Baxter came out at that moment, paused on the landing of his quarters. Shawn didn't wait for the man to speak.

"Glory—the girl. Where is she?"

Baxter wagged his head. "Gone. Pulled out a couple hours ago."

Shawn stared at the man. "Told her to wait—"

"I know you did, and I tried talking her out of

leaving. Just ain't safe for a woman by herself to be out there in the valley—but she wouldn't listen. Said she'd be all right, that there wasn't no use of her waiting around for you, and to tell you she'd gone on."

Starbuck, worry now a strong fear tearing at him, wheeled the sorrel about.

"Expect it was that load of ore she brought in," Baxter said, coming forward a few steps. "Was low-grade stuff, hardly worth working. She was plenty downhearted about it—"

Shawn raked the gelding with his spurs. With a two-hour start on him, the girl would be well up the valley, could even have reached the mine if she hadn't run into trouble. *If*—that was the catch, he thought as he sent the sorrel racing along the road.

TWENTY

With the first fan of pearl in the east, Starbuck began his search of the area around the wagon for signs that would enable him to mount a pursuit of Glory Cannon and her abductors. The probing of the nearby slopes and swales instituted earlier on the fragile hope that the girl was still in the vicinity had turned up nothing, and finally, he had abandoned the effort, dropped back to where the team had been halted, and there, restless as a caged animal, awaited the coming morning.

Bent low, stopping every few steps to investigate marks left in the rocky soil, Shawn moved around the vehicle in a gradually widening circle. He found where the wagon had been driven into the coulee, discovered that there were three riders, that the horses they rode were shod.

He felt somewhat better for that; it had not been Apaches who had taken her—at least the chances were better than good that it was not, since Indians did not shoe their mounts. Of course, there was always the possibility of an exception, as in the case of a horse stolen from some rancher that was being used by its new, coppery owner without the metal plates being removed.

It was slow going. The ground was larded with rock and covered by leaves, twigs, and sandstone shale. He experienced no difficulty in tracing the course of the wagon's entrance into the swale, but the departure of the three riders and their prisoner was a different matter.

Eventually, however, dogged persistence and patience paid off. A distance to the south of the coulee, the ever-widening circle he followed led him into a small sink. At some previous time, water from one of the infrequent rains had gathered there to form a pond. The blistering sun had soon sucked the hollow dry of moisture, and the soil had cracked and then curled into small, irregular squares and rectangles. Embedded in the crisp clay were the hoof marks of three horses.

Starbuck, grimly intent, bent over the tracks, and quickly tested the edges of the clearly defined impressions. They were fresh, had yet to disintegrate and merge into the soil.

They could have been left by none other than the kidnappers, he was certain, but he took no chances. With the sink as a starting point, he began to backtrack them to the wagon. Striking a direct line, he was able to pick up a print here and there, note a crushed or broken bush where a horse had passed, spot an overturned stone or one grazed by an iron shoe. That the riders had come from the coulee was unquestionable.

Hurriedly freeing the mules so they might forage for themselves, a task he had avoided earlier for fear they could destroy helpful signs, he mounted the sorrel and returned to the sink. The trail pointed straight for a distant bank of hills to the south and east.

He paused for a few moments, giving that thought, then decided that in the interest of time, he should gamble that the dark-looking formation was the abductor's destination and that it would be wise to hurry for that point, not spend time searching out the actual trail on the possibility that the party might change directions. If he failed to pick up the prints when he reached the hills, he would drop back, hunt until he was again on the right course.

Putting spurs to the gelding, Shawn set out at a brisk lope, eyes nevertheless scanning the ground before him for indications of the party's passage . . . Three riders. Starbuck had been too preoccupied to see any significance in that; now it came to him that there had been four outlaws who made the initial attempt at hijacking the ore. He had put one out of the running with a rifle bullet; were these three the remaining members of the original party—the same ones he had followed to Tombstone, and thanks to Parker, had lost?

It was only logical to believe so, and it was equally logical to assume they had been hired by the same person or persons who had earlier taken Ira Cannon's life and made an attempt on Glory's. Such boiled down to one thing—whoever it was now had the girl and could complete his plans to take over the mine.

Starbuck rode steadily on, with the sun now high above the eastern horizon and climbing into a clear sky. Twice he saw the prints of the outlaws' horses, once where they crossed a sandy arroyo, again where they had come off a short slope and, weight thrown to their forelegs when they leaped, left deep marks in the dark soil.

Midway across the wide prairie, he encountered two men in a buggy driving toward Tombstone, now a considerable distance to the north. The driver slowed, seemingly wishing to converse, but Shawn did not pause, simply waved a greeting, and pressed on.

He saw no more hoof prints as he drew near the brush-covered hills, and viewing the many gullies and large arroyos that gashed their slopes, an uneasiness began to grow within him. Unless he could again turn up the marks left by the horses, he would be faced with the task of searching each of the washes—and that could take hours.

Accordingly, he slowed the sorrel to a walk as they closed in on the rugged slopes and began a painstaking examination of the ground ahead of him. He had found nothing by the time he reached the first rock and brush fringe, and marking that point in his mind, he rode along the foot of the hills, continuing the search.

There was no indication of the outlaws' passage

after he had traveled a reasonable distance north, and at once he reversed directions, hurried back to where he had begun, and repeated the process on a southward course. A mile farther on, he found what he sought; three horses coming in from the flat, and falling into a single-file formation, had headed up into one of the larger canyons.

Taut, Starbuck rode quickly into the brushy cleavage as a precaution against being noticed by anyone else in the area and, guiding the sorrel into a well-hidden pocket among the rocks a safe distance from the trail, dismounted.

Picketing the horse, Shawn fell back to the faintly marked path. It followed the floor of the wash, and that it was seldom used was evidenced by the many places where it had been washed out and was cluttered with stumps and shattered tree limbs carried downstream by fierce storms, filling the arroyo with rushing rainwater.

Quiet, keeping to the side of the trail, Starbuck began the climb. The outlaws had led their horses up the bed of the wash, and their tracks along with those of their mounts were visible in an occasional stretch of soft sand. He noticed no smaller footprints, guessed Glory had been permitted to stay on a saddle to which she had probably been tied.

It was slow going through the rocks and stiff brush, made all the more so by his efforts to keep the sounds of his approach to a minimum. After a time, Shawn paused for breath, leaning against a large boulder. Almost at once, the smell of smoke drifted to him. Likely, the outlaws were making coffee, possibly cooking up a breakfast meal if they had come prepared. They could not be far away.

Starbuck resumed his climb, hands against the chunk of granite as he worked his way around its bulging side. A warning buzz brought him to a quick stop . . . Rattlesnake. He froze against the boulder. In a shallow *tinaja* on the surface of the flat rock, a big diamondback, disturbed as it lay sunning itself in the slight depression, had whipped itself into a serpentine coil.

Triangular head cocked at the end of a poised, wrist-thick body, tongue darting in and out, black and white markings pointing up the designs in its scales, the reptile regarded him with hard bead-like eyes as it challenged his presence.

Shawn rode out a long minute while the rattler continued to stare at him, the horny rattle at the tail end of its sleek body alternately issuing its threat and falling silent. To use his gun on the snake would draw the attention of the outlaws—and that was the last thing he wanted to do at that moment. A tight grin pulled at his lips.

"You win, friend," he murmured and slowly began to fade back along the boulder, making no sudden moves until he no longer faced the rattler. Once beyond the serpent's range of vision, he turned and, circling the rock, once again started to climb, keeping to the trail itself until he was well beyond the now quiet diamondback.

The odor of wood smoke became stronger. Shawn, once more in the brush edging the path, slowed his steps. A branch snapped loudly somewhere ahead, bringing him to a full stop. A voice said something—a half-dozen low spoken words, all unintelligible. Starbuck dropped into a crouch, moved on, halted.

He was at the edge of a small clearing. Beyond the fringe of brush in which he knelt was a weathered cabin, windows and doors gone, roof sagging badly. Pulled up to its side were three horses, and squatting around a fire over which a blackened coffee pot had been placed were the outlaws who had attempted to hijack the ore wagon, and that he had later followed into Tombstone.

But where was Glory Cannon?

"Ain't what I'd call it," Nate said, wagging his head.

"No? Just what would you call it?"

"Claim jumping—the hard way," the outlaw replied, and laughed.

"The permanent way," Tip corrected. "He's fixing things up so's ain't nobody ever going to be around to argue with him about who owns the place . . . You reckon it's all that good?"

"Is according to what that fellow Kruger says, but I got my doubts. That there Dutchman, Schieffelin, getting here first glommed onto all the rich stuff. Rest of the claims'll just pay a man wages and not much more. Hell, I'd rather make my pile doing something else. Digging ain't my style . . . Never did find a shovel that fit my hands."

"Well, he sure thinks that mine's worth plenty, else he wouldn't've gone to all the trouble he did."

Billy, delivering himself of that comment, rose, and started back to the mound of rocks. Halfway, he paused, cocked his head toward the trail. Shawn tensed, hearing, too, a faint rattle of gravel.

"That'll be him," Nate said. "We all loaded up so's we can take the gal and move on?"

"What's to load up?" Tip asked, dumping the remaining coffee into the fire. "We never brung nothing."

"Only the gal," Nate agreed. "Be better if we had a horse for her. This here riding double's going to slow us down plenty."

"It's all right with me," Tip said with a wide grin, and shifted his attention to the trail.

The steady thud of hooves was plain now in the still, hot air, complemented occasionally by the clatter of displaced gravel or the thump of a larger rock being overturned and falling to a lower level.

Pistol in hand, Starbuck waited tensely. There would now be four to face, but the odds were still with him; he needed only to hold off until they were together and then throw down on them. It wasn't likely anyone in the group would make a wrong move.

A horse broke into view, long head bobbing as he climbed the grade, and emerged from the brush. The man astride him took form in the shadows, then came into clear view. Surprise rocked Starbuck. The rider wasn't T. J. Yorkan as he'd expected—it was John Trimm, the assayer.

TWENTY-TWO

"Took your time getting here," Tip said sourly.

Trimm shrugged, swung off his horse. Unhooking his saddlebags draped across the horn, he tossed them to the outlaw.

"Said I'd be here by noon—I am. Where's the girl?"

Billy jerked a thumb toward the shack. "Safe inside."

"Don't want her safe," the assayer man snapped, "I want her dead."

Starbuck listened to the emotionless voice. It was hard to believe Trimm was a killer, but he had shot down Ira Cannon, according to the outlaws, and they'd have no reason not to be truthful about it. It followed that the assayer had also been the one to make the attempt on Glory's life, which had resulted in the death of Pete Lusky—and if he had not actually fired the bullet, he was responsible for it, just as he was for hiring the outlaws to kidnap the girl.

It was difficult to understand just how he would benefit from it all, however. Yorkan had good reason; if Glory failed to meet the note she'd signed when it fell due, the mine became forfeit and the property of the lawyer. How would John Trimm gain?

"Plenty of time," Tip said, rummaging about in the saddlebags. "Seems all here . . . Billy's got something he's wanting to ask."

Trimm, stiff and impatient, brushed at the sweat on his ruddy face and glanced at the outlaw. "About what?"

"Harley. Way we see it, what you're paying us now belongs to us because he wasn't in on grabbing the girl. Was in on the deal at the start, howsoever, and we figure he ought to get a little something."

"And you think I ought to pay it—"

Billy nodded.

"Forget it," Trimm said in a flat, decisive tone. "What's there is for all of you. If you want to cut Harley Gates out, it's your business . . . What're you going to do with the girl?"

Tip slung the saddlebags over his shoulder. "Taking her across the border, selling her. Can get plenty of cash for her in Nogales."

"Nogales?" the assayer repeated, and then shook his head. "Want her dead."

"Where she'll end up'll be the same as dead."

"No!" Trimm was unyielding. "Nogales is too close. Might manage to come back."

"You don't know them Mex whorehouses," Nate said, speaking up for the first time. "Once they got themselves a gal like her, they don't never let them get loose. Anyway, you got our guarantee. You won't ever lay eyes on her again."

John Trimm, a deep frown on his features, stirred irritably. "I don't like it—and I'm expecting you to live up to the deal we made—"

"Somebody's coming!"

At Billy's warning, the assayer and the other outlaws fell silent. Starbuck pulled back deeper into the brush, put his attention on the edge of the clearing where the path made its entrance. The sound that had reached Billy's ears had not been heard by him, but now the click of metal shoes against rock, the sliding of gravel, and the thud of hooves were plain.

Abruptly, Horst Kruger rode into view. Shawn stared. What had brought him to the old shack? Was it a desire to help Glory Cannon? That was it, Starbuck decided, and then it came suddenly to him: how would the engineer know where to find the girl?

Kruger, ramrod straight on the saddle of a small buckskin, a rifle hung in the crook of his arm, halted before Trimm. Ignoring the outlaws, none of whom showed any evidence of surprise, he looked steadily at the assayer.

"Followed you here."

Trimm folded his arms across his narrow chest. In the driving sunlight, the hair showing beneath his hat was a bright red.

"So?"

"Told me you weren't going to hurt Glory—the girl," Kruger said, voice trembling.

Starbuck listened, scarcely believing what he was hearing. Kruger was in on the scheme to beat Glory Cannon out of her mine, too!

"Things change," Trimm said coldly. "Had to make new plans."

"Why? Everything was going the way it was arranged. The last load of ore was of low-grade—almost worthless."

"Makes no difference. After she rung Yorkan in on it, I had to make a move. Want you to go ahead now, ship the high-grade stuff so's we can meet that note she signed. I've got the girl here. Nate and the boys are taking care of her."

Kruger's face blanked. He came off the buckskin hurriedly. "You have Glory here?" he shouted, anger forcing his accent to the surface. "I will have no part of this—and I will not let you harm her! Where is she?"

Trimm ducked his head at the shack. "In there. You sure this is what you want to do?"

Kruger nodded, and keeping the rifle leveled in the general direction of the four men, edged toward the cabin.

"You're throwing away a fortune—"

"It does not matter," the engineer mumbled. "No longer is it of importance. You can have it all. I want only to take the girl to safety and—"

"Afraid it's not that easy," Trimm cut in, his voice dry and flat. "With her alive, my claim's no good."

"I will talk with her," Kruger said, pausing before the doorway to the shack. "I will explain, and perhaps there is something that can be arranged."

"Hell with that!" Tip shouted. "There's sure something I can do!"

Starbuck lunged into the open as the outlaw whipped up his pistol.

"Tip!" he yelled and drove a bullet into the ground at the outlaw's feet.

As one, they all whirled. The weapon in Tip's hand roared. Shawn felt the slug brush hotly against his arm, and he triggered a second shot, this time at the man.

Tip stumbled backward, arms thrown wide. Billy, his pistol out, dropped to one knee. Starbuck's third bullet caught him high in the chest, knocking him flat.

"I quit!" Nate's frantic voice blended with the rolling echoes of the guns.

Shawn, crouched, forty-five leveled, nodded coldly at Trimm. "You got any ideas?"

The assayer stared at him woodenly for a long breath, and then shoulders slumping, he slowly raised his hands.

"No," he murmured.

Beyond him Horst Kruger, abandoning the rifle against the wall of the cabin, was stepping hurriedly into its shadowy interior. Starbuck, breathing deeper as the tension drained from him, crossed to where Nate and John Trimm stood. Relieving the two of them of their weapons, which he tossed into the brush, he moved back.

"Over there—against the side of the shack," he ordered.

As both men complied, he knelt beside Billy and Tip. Both were dead. Grim, he straightened up, turned to face the doorway of the cabin. Glory—features strained and white, hair in disarray, clothing dusty and torn—came suddenly into the open, hesitated briefly, and then ran to him. Behind her, Horst Kruger halted, eyes down.

"Oh, Shawn!" she cried. "I'm so glad you came! I—I was afraid I'd never see you again!"

Starbuck remained motionless as the girl's arms went around him. "It's all over now," he said quietly.

"I hope so," she sobbed, "and I hope you'll never leave me. I don't want you to ever go away."

With his free hand, Starbuck gently disengaged himself. "We'll not go through that again, Glory," he said sternly, and added, "you all right?"

The girl drew back, face tipped down. "I guess so—"

Starbuck raised a hand and beckoned to Kruger. The engineer crossed the clearing with dragging steps, and when Shawn pointed, he took a place alongside Trimm and Nate.

"You belong with them, seems."

Kruger nodded heavily. Starbuck felt the girl's eyes suddenly upon him.

"Was Horst a part of it?"

Shawn nodded. "Figured you'd heard them talking—"

"I did—a part of it, but I didn't understand."

"He was in with Trimm. I had my mind set on it being Yorkan, but I was wrong. It was those two—and these outlaws they'd hired to do the work for them."

"I just can't believe that Horst would—"

"Fooled me, too, but no more than Trimm did. Never once figured it'd be him—and I still don't savvy why. Expect right now would be a good time to find out."

Starbuck moved away from the girl, drew up close to the three men ranged along the wall of the cabin.

"Since there's no marshal in Tombstone to turn you over to, means I'll have to take the law into my own hands," he said coolly.

Trimm's head came up abruptly. "You can't—"

"Best you wait and see. I've got a good rope on my saddle. Aim to take you one at a time, string you up unless I get the answers I'm looking for. Anybody want to speak up?"

There was a long minute of sullen silence, and then Horst Kruger said, "I will talk."

TWENTY-THREE

Kruger seemed to take a firm grip upon himself. Facing Glory, he said, "I will tell you this, your claim is a good one, maybe one of the best in these hills. The ore that I sent to the mill for you was of low grade, of little worth—"

"Why?" Glory was staring at him fixedly, lips tightly compressed.

"It was on purpose that I did so. The high-grade ore, of which there will be plenty, is rich and will bring you perhaps ten thousand dollars a ton."

"But—why?" the girl repeated.

"It was to make you think the mine was worthless. That was the arrangement I had with Trimm, and when we got you to where you'd be willing to quit, then we were going to take over and work the claim very hard. I was to own one-third; Trimm, the balance. It was his estimate that we would take one million dollars' worth of silver from the claim."

"If you only planned to freeze out Glory, why did you try to kill her?" Starbuck asked, his voice harsh.

"It was not my idea. The fact is that her father getting killed and the shot that was taken at her happened before I made a partnership with Trimm."

Shawn shifted his attention to the assayer. "Was

all your doing, then, but it don't make any sense. Can't see how you'd gain. You could get your hands on her mine by buying her out—but to kill her—"

"You don't get anything from me," Trimm muttered, shaking his head.

"Well, you do from me!" Nate said. "Hell, mister, we was just hired to do a job—me and Tip and Billy and Harley Gates. Can't blame us for—"

"You've got plenty to answer for," Starbuck snapped. "Just because you were hired to do what you've done, won't let you off—"

"It is clear now what happened," Kruger said thoughtfully, as if not hearing anyone else. "The signing of that note of Yorkan's was what forced Trimm's hand. It was necessary that we at once take possession of the mine and ship enough good ore to pay off the loan. If we continued to ship only the low-grade, we would defeat ourselves. Such was why he decided to—"

"He decided? You saying you weren't in on their kidnapping Glory?"

The engineer shrugged. "No. When you told me of the attack on the wagon, I could not understand. I told myself perhaps it was only outlaws hoping to rob you of ore. But as I worked and I think of it and I learn from you what the outlaws look like, I realized that they were the men Trimm hired to do jobs for him.

"So, after you and Glory left for the mill with that second load, I went to Tombstone to talk with Trimm and insist that he stand by his promise to not harm Glory. I could not find him, but this morning I learned that he had been seen riding south, so I rented a horse and followed," Kruger hesitated, turned apologetically to the girl. "Believe me, I did not know they had made of you a prisoner. I—I am sorry."

She looked away, coldly ignoring him. Shawn, still unsatisfied, said, "Haven't got this straight in my head yet. Can maybe understand why Trimm would want Ira Cannon out of the way, but Glory—"

Kruger glanced at the assayer, as if expecting him to make a reply. When none was forthcoming, he shrugged.

"It is like this," he said. "Trimm staked Ira Cannon, and when Cannon made his strike, he not only paid off the money he had borrowed, but to show his gratitude, he willed the mine to Trimm in case anything happened to him—and if his daughter did not come to claim it.

"Cannon was not sure his daughter was alive. He had not heard of her for years, so he sent a letter to where she had lived soon after he'd made his strike—"

"I never got any letter," Glory said, coming back around.

Shawn nodded. "Figuring the time, it probably

got to Wickenburg about the day you reached Tombstone."

"There is a paper, a sort of will," Kruger continued, "that Trimm has. It states that the mine is his property if the daughter does not appear within six months."

It was all clear now to Starbuck; with the girl out of the way, Ira Cannon's mine belonged to John Trimm. It was that simple.

"Don't know how the law in Tucson will figure all this," he said, placing his attention on the three men, "but murder's murder, and I expect that's what you all will be charged with—leastwise you, Trimm, and your friend Nate. May be different for you, Kruger. I'll tell the sheriff you weren't in on the killing of Ira Cannon and that you tried to stop them from doing anything to Glory."

Only the engineer made any response, nodding heavily.

"First thing will be to get you back to Tombstone, look up Yorkan. I owe him an apology, and then I want his advice as to what I ought to do—"

"I'll tell you what you best do," a voice drawled from the brush at the edge of the clearing. "You'd best raise your hands unless you want me to blow your head off."

Starbuck froze, wheeled slowly. From behind him, Nate shouted, "Harley—I'm sure glad to see you!"

It was the fourth outlaw. Pistol cocked and leveled, a dirty bandage wrapped about his chest visible beneath an unbuttoned shirt, he looked pale and haggard.

"Figured I'd best come collect my share of the pay. Weren't for certain one of you'd be bringing it to me." He flicked the bodies of Tip and Billy with his feverish eyes. "What's been going on?"

Starbuck studied the outlaw closely. The man was unsteady on his feet and seemed about to cave in. The wound he had sustained had weakened him badly, and the long ride from Tombstone had aggravated his condition.

"Put away that gun," he said. "You'll never be able to leave here, shape you're in."

"The hell he won't!" Nate shouted, pulling away from the side of the shack and hurrying across the clearing to where Gates stood. "I'm going to be taking over for him."

"And don't horse around with this jasper," Trimm added, also regaining his presence of mind and stepping clear of the cabin. "Put a bullet in him—and take care of the girl and Kruger, too. Want this thing cleaned up here and now. Got a million dollars at stake and I don't want anything screwing it up."

Shawn, poised, watched Nate, halted beside Harley Gates, reach for the pistol in the man's hand, take it from him. It was now—or never at all.

"Nate!" he yelled and drew fast.

The outlaw triggered his weapon as Starbuck fired. The shots blended as one, setting up a chain of echoes rocking through the hills.

Nate spun half around and went to his knees. Shawn, untouched, spun to face John Trimm. The assayer, a perplexed look on his ruddy features, was staring at the fallen outlaw. Both hands were pressed to his middle, and blood was oozing from between his fingers.

"Nate . . . you damned fool . . . you've missed him . . . hit me," he mumbled in an angry, halting voice and abruptly collapsed.

"Harley Gates is dead—"

The announcement from T. J. Yorkan came as no surprise to Starbuck. The outlaw's wound—serious at the outset, all but completely neglected by him, and further complicated by the hard ride he'd made to the shack—had finally overcome him.

They had all gathered on the following day in the back-room office, the lawyer occasionally made use of. Everything had been settled and arranged, and as Glory's representative, he had made it clear he was taking charge.

"Leaves only you," he said crisply, turning his attention to Horst Kruger. "Pretty serious matter that—"

"I'm forgetting about what he did," Glory cut

in, "and hiring him to run the mine for me."

Yorkan frowned. A smile spread across Kruger's face. "Thank you," he said in a grateful voice. "I will do my—"

Still cold to the engineer, Glory swung questioningly to Starbuck. "Are you going to ride on?"

Shawn, the two hundred dollars he'd earned and that had been paid to him by Yorkan at the girl's instructions heavy in his pocket, nodded.

"Pulling out for Bisbee. Good chance my brother might be there."

"There's a bigger chance he won't," she snapped. "Are you going to go on forever like this—throwing your life away, denying your own self and people who—"

She broke off suddenly, looked down. Starbuck was silent for a long minute listening to the tumult in the streets, only slightly muted by the walls of the building.

"You know where I stood from the start," he said finally, and moved toward the door. Pausing there, he glanced back and smiled briefly. "So long—and good luck," he added as he stepped out into the dust-laden sunlight.

ABOUT THE AUTHOR

Ray Hogan inspired a loyal following over the years after he published his first Western novel, *Ex-Marshal*, in 1956. Hogan was born in Willow Springs, Missouri, where his father was town marshal. When Hogan was five years old, the family moved to Albuquerque, where they lived in the foothills of the Sandia and Manzano Mountains. His father was on the Albuquerque police force and, in later years, owned the Overland Hotel. It was while listening to his father and other old-timers tell tales from the past that Ray was inspired to recast these tales in fiction. From the beginning, he did exhaustive research into the history and the people of the Old West, and the walls of his study were lined with various pictures, books, firearms, spurs, and memorabilia, about all of which he could talk in dramatic detail. "I've attempted to capture the courage and bravery of those men and women who lived out West, and the dangers and problems they had to overcome," Hogan once remarked. Above all, what is most impressive about Hogan's Western novels is the consistent quality with which each is crafted, the compelling depth of his characters, and his ability to juxtapose the complexities of human conflict into narratives always as intensely interesting as they are emotionally involving.

Center Point Large Print
600 Brooks Road / PO Box 1
Thorndike, ME 04986-0001 USA

(207) 568-3717

US & Canada:
1 800 929-9108
www.centerpointlargeprint.com